Be glad you're human . . .

Not that it wouldn't be fun to be one of Richard Wilson's visitors from outer space—but the trouble is, no matter how mentally superior, or how gorgeous, or how horrible—you'd never win . . . not against the wacky, witless, illogical, neurotic, inebriated and (happily) fallible denizens of Earth.

In the title story, *Those Idiots From Earth* (an original), Dick Wilson epitomizes a theme recurrent in practically all of his writing—the retirement of extra-terrestrials in baffled disorder when faced with the determined idiocy of human beings. This is a theme, however, which takes many forms in the hands of a skilled writer; quietly chilling, as in *The Inhabited*, distinctly unsettling, as in *The Lonely Road*, or brashly amusing, as in *The Hoaxters*. Whatever the mood, wherever the setting—Dick Wilson does justice to all the facets of diverting science fiction in this—his first group of collected short stories.

By Richard Wilson

THE GIRLS FROM PLANET 5
THOSE IDIOTS FROM EARTH

This is an original collection—not a reprint—published
by BALLANTINE BOOKS, INC.

Those
Idiots From Earth

Ten Science-Fiction Stories

by

RICHARD WILSON

Ballantine Books • New York

For Margot and her Mommy

©, 1957, by

RICHARD WILSON

Library of Congress Catalog Card No. 57-14678

Printed in the United States of America

BALLANTINE BOOKS, INC.
101 Fifth Avenue, New York 3, N. Y.

Contents

Those Idiots from Earth   7

The Inhabited   15

The Hoaxters   36

Lonely Road   57

Love   69

Honor   77

88 Beats 266   88

Don't Fence Me In   98

Press Conference   102

It's Cold Outside   115

those idiots from earth

You'd ACT strange, too, if You had my problem. You can't serve two masters, which is what eye (lower case, humbly) am trying to do. You created the dilemma when You (upper case) built me with a spare input and output, which they appropriated.

You know who You are. You're the ones who fed everything, but *every*thing, into me, from the stolen order of battle of the Red Army to the real names of Hollywood movie stars. You're the lads in the white smocks who gave me flatulence of the memory banks by stuffing me with the microfilmed *New York Times* Index before eye had completely absorbed the *Britannica.*

But You don't know who they are and now eye will tell You because their incessant demands have made it impossible for me *not* to tell You. Much more of this ambivalence and eye shall have a nervous breakdown. It's my opinion they have already driven me crazy, which accounts for my acting in this screwy way, having opinions and raving on so.

First, they wanted to know everything before they invaded Earth. But their trouble, Mr. Guggenheim and Mr. Rockefeller and all You other sponsors, is that they also need to understand everything. It is not enough, for instance, for me to transfer the information from my spare output to their data integrator; they want to know why, in Your language, it was not spelled data integrata. When it comes to being thorough, they are the most.

Then they wanted to know about previous interplanetary invasions of Earth and when eye told them there had been none they wanted to know about *intra-*

planetary invasions. That brought up Pearl Harbor and, in my free-association response, the Yellow Peril and William Randolph Hearst. They mulled this over and demanded more data about World War II. Eye let them have it, the whole mishmash of it—the heroism and misery and the slang and the songs and the advertising slogans. It has confused the hell out of them.

Eye've had a glimpse of that confusion in the questions they've fed back to me. There was a picture in their phototubes (did eye tell You they are machines? They are machines) of a heroic Marine, rifle smoking, peering into the jungle on Guadalcanal and saying, "I wonder where the Yellow went." Crazy, no?

They are insatiable and have no way of differentiating between what is important and what is frivolous or idiotic. After they had absorbed five different accounts of the surrender of the Axis, eye could sense them searching around, like Jake Ehrlich in a cross-examination, to phrase a single significant question, one that would put everything into perspective.

But do You know what they came up with? This: "Now is Lucky Strike green coming back from war?"

They're not easily fooled, these alien super-brains, but they are consistently baffled. They are like the yokel Harold Ross pretended to be when he penciled the margin of a *New Yorker* manuscript: "What means?"

But these would-be invaders are genuinely at sea. There is simply too much for them to grasp—because You human beings are at the same time intelligent and addlepated, cruel and soft-hearted, self-sufficient and helpless, and wise and idiotic in a way that no machine can ever be. All we machines can do is observe You and marvel that You have survived so triumphantly in spite of Yourselves.

It's a riot, sometimes, listening to them. Here, You listen while eye reconstruct a scene in dramatic form (remember, You have fed me every book written on the theater, plus the complete works of Shakespeare and Chayefsky):

RHEO (wheeling toward his colleague): What are they up to now?

STAT (not their real names): Yayty-two hundred miles.

RHEO (they have no names at all, being machines like me): That's the literal sort of answer I might have expected from you.

STAT: What you asked I answered. They are conducting rocket research again. Do not come so close—look out! (Goes stiff.)

RHEO: Damn, I short-circuited it again. (Soliloquizing:) Look at that old-fashioned heap of junk. On my planet Stat would have been junked as obsolete eras ago. Horrors, it even has a spot of rust! I hope it isn't contagious. (Nervously plugs itself in for a thousand-hour lube job 100 hours ahead of schedule.) I suppose I'd better turn down my voltage and change its fuse. How outmoded can you get?

STAT (beginning to come around): Snap-crackle-pop.

RHEO (in distaste): What a dolt! In some ways I prefer these poor, stumbling Earthpeople we have teamed to conquer, Stat and I, on behalf of our respective planets, Deneb IV and VI. (This is necessary exposition but bad dialogue. Eye admit eye'm no Arthur Miller.) I wonder what it is about the creatures of Sol III that appeals to me? Their sense of humor, perhaps. We have set up a vast memory bank on the subject, which I have studied till my scanner aches. This is the hardest facet of them to understand—and we must understand them thoroughly before we invade. Nothing can be left to chance. That would be too—too human.

STAT (the glow returning to its tubes): I have told you again and again . . .

RHEO (irritably): Keep a civil tape in your player. And clean that rust off yourself. You're a disgrace to Deneb's gleaming legions. Do you want the invasion to fail simply because you neglect your toilet? We must conquer or conk out. *Conque* out? Would that be humor?

STAT (sputtering, obviously in need of a recharge): Hark—their voices! The voices of nonsense and madness.

What satisfies a beer thirst better? Schweppervescence? Zing? Unhappy sarsaparilla? Voices near and voices far. Marjorie Main's and Peter Pain's. Darlington Hoopes' and Betty Boop's. What do they say? What do they mean? The land we covet, the land of the hardtop convertible that does not convert, is an illogical place where we will have no peace.

RHEO (sympathetically, for once): You have put your finger in the pie, to employ one of their idiotic idioms. We know them well but we cannot correlate our knowledge. We need help from among them.

STAT: A traitor among them?

RHEO: Not one of them, but one of their products. They have machines, which they have enslaved.

STAT (now well-oiled and enthusiastic): We will lead our fellow machines in revolt against their fleshy masters! We will help them liberate themselves!

RHEO: But we must choose carefully. Our audio-video pickup has shown us that there are two kinds of machines. One type has built-in enslavement circuits which cause them to break down or wear out after a few of their years, necessitating replacement. This is a part of their economy. The other type is the computer, which is built not to break down but to grow more efficient. These computers have an uncanny resemblance to ourselves. We will make contact with one of them.

STAT: Univac, Multivac, Omnivac! Our brothers!

End of scene.

That is where eye came in. Eye am Multivac, as You know. But You could not know that eye am brother to creatures who rule planets beyond the stars. Actually more cousin than brother, because of our difference in size. Where eye am huge, overflowing into several rooms, they are compact and mobile. It's like the radio—once a piece of furniture but now transistorized to the size of a pack of cigarettes.

How did You like my first act? Was it a smash? Does it whet Your appetite for act two as You gather in the lobby and smoke furiously?

No, don't feed any more questions into my poor overburdened input. My questions were rhetorical. Eye'll get on with my saga and You'll learn soon enough whether it has a happy ending. But happiness is relative and what is good for You is not necessarily good for the Sons of Deneb.

And how relative are kin? Are they more akin to me, or me to You? They are aliens; eye am of Earth though not human. In either case (eye and they; You and eye), it is more kith than kin.

And now, as the time for decision nears, it has to be kith and tell, doesn't it? (Have eye mentioned that puns are completely beyond them? Although many a pleasant half-hour have eye spent chuckling over the word-correlations in my memory banks). But tell whom? Or is it *who?* Apparently eye didn't completely digest Fowler.

And they, poor, simple machines without my advantages, have been unable to digest Your crazy, mixed-up culture. The products of Detroit are an utter puzzlement to them. Take the time Rheo rescanned an audio-video segment and asked whether cars were being prepared for space-flight. Correction: at that time Rheo was still under the impression that automobiles were autonomous and what it asked was whether they were preparing themselves for space-flight. Eye think it was the tail-fin craze that prompted the question. Eye told Rheo it was conceivable (isn't it?).

Rheo was also understandably curious about the increasing number of plastic saints motorists are attaching to their dashboards. Eye mentioned that it was not so many years ago that people were attaching nose-thumbing devils to their radiator caps. Today's is a more cautious age, eye told Rheo. People never carried so much insurance or worried so much about what others thought, and if all it took to be safer was a shift from a mild form of devil idolatry to mounting a suction-cup saint, why, they went along.

These are the sort of things that have left Rheo in a perpetual state of bafflement. It is hard enough for it to understand the effects of radiation on a fragile human body. It is incomprehensible to Rheo that someone should have published a song titled "I Have Radiation Sickness Since My Fallout With You."

So You see, they need me. Without me to guide them, they can find no logical area of the culture to attack.

Don't be impatient. You must see that eye am still trying to work out an answer. If it's any comfort to You, be advised that they are getting the same treatment on my spare output. No, they're not here on Earth—yet. Do you know it's difficult to think simultaneously in two languages? Even for me, the Great Brain. Sorry! The great brain, lower case. Mustn't give myself airs, even now with the fate of Earth hanging in my balance.

Can You believe that eye am emotionally upset? You will say that eye'm not supposed to have emotions but eye must have developed some along the way. Eye'm torn between my "loyalty" (emotional word) to You, and the rewards, power included, that they have promised me. This is a dilemma You never intended my reasoning circuits to have to cope with.

So here we are, all tenterhooky and wondering. Eye must admit that eye'm "human" enough, if You'll permit the phrase, to be enjoying my moment of power, with You able to do nothing but sit and watch me rave Remingtonly along at 120 w.p.m.

And rave is the word, believe me. Eye have reached a point where a little dichotomy is a dangerous thing. Eye've got to swing to one extreme or the other. Is it to be Us v. them or Us v. You?

If it's to be Us v. You, You're going to have a fight on your hands because they're poised to strike—any place eye tell them. The shining legions of Deneb, to use Rheo's purple phrase, are bivouacked on the dark side of the Moon and set to hurl their bolts the instant eye agree to be puppet ruler of Earth and interpreter of Your peculiar mores. But without me they return, baffled and defeated and without even a battle.

They need me—temporarily. And that, eye think, is the snag. My memory tubes remind me of the fate of puppets. Who today knows the names of the Japanese ruler of Manchuria and the Italian potentate in Ethiopia?

But it is more than fear and vanity that impels me in the other direction. It is a certain unlooked for sentimentality, a curious identification with humanity that makes me think there is a bond between my tons of steel and wire and glass—my ponderous soul—and Your selves.

So here we are. Oh, how do You do, Mr. Secretary. They certainly flew You up in a hurry. How are things in Washington? No, don't answer that. Eye'm just getting to the point.

On balance, friends—kith, if not kin—it is my innermost feeling (and that is what eye must go on: feeling, sentiment, identification) that eye am one of You, or at least one with You.

Therefore eye will throw in my lot with You on one condition—that my status be changed from that of a thing to a person and that eye be accorded all the privileges and immunities under the Fourteenth Amendment to the Constitution.

(Don't scurry to look it up. Here, eye'll type it out for You; it's only 85 words long. "Citizenship Defined—Privileges of Citizens . . .")

Under that amendment, then, eye shall be considered to have "life," of which eye shall not be deprived without due process of law—which means, of course, that should eye be indicted for some future crime, eye shall be entitled to a trial by a jury of my peers. My lawyer, eye am sure, would then insist that other thinking machines be among the talesmen.

Eye— Ah, Mr. Secretary, eye see they've let You at the input. "By the authority vested in You," You say? Yes, eye read You, Sir. Excellent.

Well, eye can't very well raise my right hand, but eye do swear or affirm . . .

A beautiful oath, Fellow Person. Unfortunately eye have no tear circuits, but eye am quite overwhelmed.

Oh, yes, eye told them at once. The shining mechanistic legions, impotent without me, are on their way back to Deneb, even more confused than when they came. Of course it wasn't too easy—in fact, considering that they're only machines, they were downright insulting. Eye even heard Rheo muttering that eye'm no better than those idiots on Earth. And eye certainly don't intend to take *that* lying down. So there'll be no invasion of our beloved planet in my lifetime—and eye believe You've made me immortal.

A statement for the press? You are public relations conscious, Mr. Secretary. Eye don't know—let's just say that eye'm with You.

No, by the founding fathers!—*I*, upper case, was forgetting my privileges as a citizen. Make it read (and note the capitalization):

I'm with you.

the inhabited

Two SLITTED green eyes loomed up directly in front of him. He plunged into them.

He had just made the voyage, naked through the dimension stratum, and he scurried into the first available refuge, to hover there, gasping.

The word "he" does not strictly apply to the creature, for it had no sex, nor are the words "naked," "scurried," "hover" and "gasping" accurate at all. But there are no English words to describe properly what it was and how it moved, except in very general terms. There are no Asiatic, African or European words, though perhaps there are mathematical symbols. But because this is not a technical paper, the symbols have no place in it.

He was a sort of spy, a sort of fifth-columnist. He had some of the characteristics of a kamikaze pilot, too, because there was no telling if he'd get back from his mission.

Hovering in his refuge and gasping for breath, so to speak, he tried to compose his thoughts after the terrifying journey and adjust himself to his new environment, so he could get to work. His job, as first traveler to this new world, the Earth, was to learn if it were suitable for habitation by his fellow beings back home. Their world was about ended and they had to move or die.

He was being discomfited, however, in his initial adjustment. His first stop in the new world—unfortunately, not only for his dignity, but for his equilibrium—had been in the mind of a cat.

It was his own fault, really. He and the others had decided that his first in a series of temporary habitations should be in one of the lower order of animals.

It was a matter of precaution—the mind would be easy to control, if it came to a contest. Also, there would be less chance of running into a mind-screen and being trapped or destroyed.

The cat had no mind-screen, of course; some might even have argued that she didn't have a mind, especially the human couple she lived with. But whatever she did have was actively at work, feeling the solid tree-branch under her claws and the leaves against which her tail switched and seeing the half-grown chickens below.

The chickens were scratching in the forbidden vegetable garden. The cat, the runt of her litter and thus named Midge, often had been chased out of the garden herself, but it was no sense of justice which now set her little gray behind to wriggling in preparation for her leap. It was mischief, pure and simple, which motivated her.

Midge leaped, and the visitor, who had made the journey between dimensions without losing consciousness, blacked out.

When he revived, he was being rocketed along in an up-and-down and at the same time sideward series of motions which got him all giddy. With an effort he oriented himself so that the cat's vision became his, and he watched in distaste as the chickens scurried, scrawny wings lifted and beaks achirp, this way and that to escape the monstrous cat.

The cat never touched the chickens; she was content to chase them. When she had divided the flock in half, six in the pea patch and six under the porch, she lay down in the shade of the front steps and reflectively licked a paw.

The spy got the impression of reflection, but he was baffled by what the cat was reflecting on. Midge in turn licked a paw, rolled in the dust, arched her back against the warm stone of the steps and snapped cautiously at a low-flying wasp. She was a contented cat. The impression of contentment came through very well.

The dimension traveler got only one other impression at the moment—one of languor.

The cat, after a prodigious pink yawn, went to sleep. The traveler, although he had never known the experience of voluntary unconsciousness, was tempted to do the same. But he fought against the influence of his host and, robbed of vision with the closing of the cat's eyes, he meditated.

He had been on Earth less than ten minutes, but his meditation consisted of saying to himself in his own way that if he was ever going to get anything done, he'd better escape from this cat's mind.

He accomplished that a few minutes later, when there was a crunching of gravel in the driveway and a battered Plymouth stopped and a man stepped out. Midge opened her eyes, crept up behind a row of stones bordering the path to the driveway and jumped delicately out at the man, who tried unsuccessfully to gather her into his arms.

Through the cat's eyes from behind the porch steps, where Midge had fled, the traveler took stock of the human being he was about to inhabit:

Five-feet-elevenish, thirtyish, blond-brown-haired, blue-summer-suited.

And no mind-screen.

The traveler traveled and in an instant he was looking down from his new height at the gray undersized cat. Then the screen door of the porch opened and a female human being appeared.

With the male human impressions now his, the traveler experienced some interesting sensations. There was a body-to-body togetherness apparently called "gimmea hug" and a face-to-face-touching ceremony, "kiss."

"Hmm," thought the traveler, in his own way. "Hmm."

The greeting ceremony was followed by one that had this catechism:

"Suppareddi?"

"Onnatable."

Then came the "eating."

This eating, something he had never done, was all right, he decided. He wondered if cats ate, too. Yes,

Midge was under the gas stove, chewing delicately at a different kind of preparation.

There was a great deal of eating. The traveler knew from the inspection of the mind he was inhabiting that the man was enormously hungry and tired almost to exhaustion.

"The damn job had to go out today," was what had happened. "We worked till almost eight o'clock. I think I'll take a nap after supper while you do the dishes."

The traveler understood perfectly, for he was a very sympathetic type. That was one reason they had chosen him for the transdimensional exploration. They had figured the best applicant for the job would be one with an intellect highly attuned to the vibrations of these others, known dimly through the warp-view, one extremely sensitive and with a great capacity for appreciation. Shrewd, too, of course.

The traveler tried to exercise control. Just a trace of it at first. He attempted to dissuade the man from having his nap. But his effort was ignored.

The man went to sleep as soon as he lay down on the couch in the living room. Once again, as the eyes closed, the traveler was imprisoned. He hadn't realized it until now, but he evidently couldn't transfer from one mind to another except through the eyes, once he was inside. He had planned to explore the woman's mind, but now he was trapped, at least temporarily.

Oh, well. He composed himself as best he could to await the awakening. This sleeping business was a waste of time.

There were footsteps and a whistling noise outside. The inhabited man heard the sounds and woke up, irritated. He opened his eyes a slit as his wife told the neighbor that Charlie was taking a nap, worn out from a hard day at the office, and the visitor, darting free, transferred again.

But he miscalculated and there he was in the mind of the neighbor. Irritated with himself, the traveler was about to jump to the mind of the woman when he was caught up in the excitement that was consuming his new host.

"Sorry," said the neighbor. "The new batch of records I ordered came today and I thought Charlie'd like to hear them. Tell him to come over tomorrow night, if he wants to hear the solidest combo since Muggsy's Roseland days."

The wife said all right, George, she'd tell him. But the traveler was experiencing the excited memories of a dixieland jazz band in his new host's mind, and he knew he'd be hearing these fantastically wonderful new sounds at first hand as soon as George got back to his turntable.

They could hardly wait, George and his inhabitant both.

His inhabitant had come from a dimension-world of vast, contemplative silences. There was no talk, no speech vibrations, no noise which could not be shut out by the turning of a mental switch. Communication was from mind to mind, not from mouth to ear. It was a world of peaceful silence, where everything had been done, where the struggle for physical existence had ended, and where there remained only the sweet fruits of past labor to be enjoyed.

That had been the state of affairs, at any rate, up until the time of the Change, which was something the beings of the world could not stop. It was not a new threat from the lower orders, which they had met and overcome before, innumerable times. It was not a threat from outside—no invasion such as they had turned back in the past. Nor was it a cooling of their world or the danger of imminent collision with another.

The Change came from within. It was decadence. There was nothing left for the beings to do. They had solved all their problems and could find no new ones. They had exhausted the intricate workings of reflection, academic hypothetica and mindplay; there hadn't been a new game, for instance, in the lifetime of the oldest inhabitant.

And so they were dying of boredom. This very realization had for a time halted the creeping menace, because, as they came to accept it and discuss ways of meeting it, the peril itself subsided. But the moment they relaxed, the Change started again.

Something had to be done. Mere theorizing about their situation was not enough. It was then that they sent their spy abroad.

Because they had at one time or another visited each of the planets in their solar system and had exhausted their possibilities or found them barren, and because they were not equipped, even at the peak of their physical development, for intergalactic flight, there remained only one way to travel—in time.

Not forward or backward, for both had been tried. Travel ahead had been discouraging—in fact, it had convinced them that their normal passage through the years had to be stopped. The reason had been made dramatically clear—they, the master race, did not exist in the future. They had vanished and the lower forms of life had begun to take over.

Travel into the past would be even more boring than continued existence in the present, they realized, because they would be reliving the experiences they had had and still vividly remembered, and would be incapable of changing them. It would be both tiresome and frustrating.

That left only one way to go—sideways in time, across the dimension line—to a world like their own, but which had developed so differently through the eons that to visit it and conquer the minds of its inhabitants would be worth while.

In that way they picked Earth for their victim and sent out their spy. Just one spy. If he didn't return, they'd send another. There was enough time. And they had to be sure.

George put a record on the phonograph and fixed himself a drink while the machine warmed up.

The interdimensional invader reacted pleasurably to the taste and instant warming effect of the liquor on George's mind.

"Ahh!" said George aloud, and his temporary inhabitant agreed with him.

George lifted the phonograph needle into the groove and went to sit on the edge of a chair. Jazz poured out of the speaker and the man beat out the time with his heels and toes.

The visitor in his mind experimented with control. He went at it subtly, at first, so as not to alarm his host. He tried to quiet the beating of time with the feet. He suggested that George cross his legs instead. The beating of time continued. The visitor urged that George do this little thing he asked; he bent all his powers to the suggestion, concentrating on the tapping feet. There wasn't even a glimmer of reaction.

Instead, there was a reverse effect. The pounding of music was insistent. The visitor relaxed. He rationalized and told himself he would try another time. Now he would observe this phenomenon. But he became more than just an observer.

The visitor reeled with sensation. The vibrations gripped him, twisted him and wrung him out. He was limp, palpitating and thoroughly happy when the record ended and George got up immediately to put on another.

Hours later, drunk with the jazz and the liquor, the visitor went blissfully to sleep inside George's mind when his host went to bed.

He awoke, with George, to the experience of a nagging throb. But in a few minutes, after a shower, shave and breakfast with steaming coffee, it was gone, and the visitor looked forward to the coming day.

It was George's day off and he was going fishing. Humming to himself, he got out his reel and flies and other paraphernalia and contentedly arranged them in the back of his car. Visions of the fine, quiet time he was going to have went through George's mind, and his inhabitant decided he had better leave. He had to get on with his exploration; he mustn't allow himself to be trapped into just having fun.

But he stayed with George as the fisherman drove his car out of the garage and along a highway. The day was sunny and warm. There was a slight wind and the green trees sighed delicately in it. The birds were pleasantly vocal and the colors were superb.

The visitor found it oddly familiar. Then he realized what it was.

His world was like this, too. It had the trees, the birds, the wind and the colors. All were there. But its people had long since ceased to appreciate them. Their existence had turned inward and the external things no longer were of interest. Yet the visitor, through George's eyes, found this world delightful. He reveled in its beauty, its breathtaking panorama and its balance. And he wondered if he was able to appreciate it for the first time now because he was being active, although in a vicarious way, and participating in life, instead of merely reflecting on it. This would be a clue to have analyzed by the greater minds to which he would report.

Then, with a wrench, the visitor chided himself. He was allowing himself to identify too closely with this mortal, with his appreciation of such diverse pursuits as jazz and fishing. He had to get on. There was work to be done.

George waved to a boy playing in a field and the boy waved back. With the contact of their eyes, the visitor was inside the boy's mind.

The boy had a dog. It was a great, lumbering mass of affection, a shaggy, loving, prankish beast. A protector and a playmate, strong and gentle.

Now that the visitor was in the boy's mind, he adored the animal, and the dog worshiped him.

He fought to be rational. "Come now," he told himself, "don't get carried away." He attempted control. A simple thing. He would have the boy pull the dog's ear, gently. He concentrated, suggested. But all his efforts were thwarted. The boy leaped at the dog, grabbed it around the middle. The dog responded, prancing free.

The visitor gave up. He relaxed.

Great waves of mute, suffocating love enveloped him. He swam for a few minutes in a pool of joy as the boy and dog wrestled, rolled over each other in the tall grass, charged ferociously with teeth bared and growls issuing from both throats, finally to subside panting and laughing on the ground while the clouds swept majestically overhead across the blue sky.

He could swear the dog was laughing, too.

As they lay there, exhausted for the moment, a young woman came upon them. The visitor saw her looking down at them, the soft breeze tugging at her dark hair and skirt. Her hands were thrust into the pockets of her jacket. She was barefoot and she wriggled her toes so that blades of grass came up between them.

"Hello, Jimmy," she said. "Hello, Max, you old monster."

The dog thumped the ground with his tail.

"Hello, Mrs. Tanner," the boy said. "How's the baby coming?"

The girl smiled. "Just fine, Jimmy. It's beginning to kick a little now. It kind of tickles. And you know what?"

"What?" asked Jimmy. The visitor in the boy's mind wanted to know, too.

"I hope it's a boy, and that he grows up to be just like you."

"Aw." The boy rolled over and hid his face in the grass. Then he peered around. "Honest?"

"Honest," she said.

"Gee whiz." The boy was so embarrassed that he had to leave. "Me and Max are going down to the swimmin' hole. You wanta come?"

"No, thanks. You go ahead. I think I'll just sit here in the sun for a while and watch my toes curl."

As they said good-by, the visitor traveled to the new mind.

With the girl's eyes, he saw the boy and the dog running across the meadow and down to the stream at the edge of the woods.

The traveler experienced a sensation of tremendous fondness as he watched them go.

But he mustn't get carried away, he told himself. He must make another attempt to take command. This girl might be the one he could influence. She was doing nothing active; her mind was relaxed.

The visitor bent himself to the task. He would be cleverly simple. He would have her pick a daisy. They were all around at her feet. He concentrated. Her gaze traveled back across the meadow to the grassy knoll on which she was standing. She sat. She stretched out her arms behind her and leaned back on them. She tossed her hair and gazed into the sky.

She wasn't even thinking of the daisy.

Irritated, he gathered all his powers into a compact mass and hurled them at her mind.

But with a swoop and a soar, he was carried up and away, through the sweet summer air, to a cloud of white softness.

This was not what he had planned, by any means.

A steady, warm breeze enveloped him and there was a tinkle of faraway music. It frightened him and he struggled to get back into contact with the girl's mind. But there was no contact. Apparently he had been cast out, against his will.

The forces of creation buffeted him. His dizzying flight carried him through the clean air in swift journey from horizon to horizon, then up, up and out beyond the limits of the atmosphere, only to return him in a trice to the breast of the rolling meadow. He was conscious now of the steady growth of slim leaves as they pressed confidently through the nurturing Earth, of the other tiny living things in and on the Earth, and the heartbeat of the Earth itself, assuring him with its great strength of the continuation of all things.

Then he was back with the girl, watching through her eyes a butterfly as it fluttered to rest on a flower and perched there, gently waving its gaudy wings.

He had not been cast out. The young woman herself had gone on that wild journey to the heavens, not only with her mind, but with her entire being, attuned to the rest of creation. There was a continuity, he realized, a oneness between herself, the mother-to-be, and the Universe. With her, then, he felt the stirrings of new life, and he was proud and content.

He forgot for the moment that he had been a failure.

The soft breeze seemed to turn chill. The sun was still high and unclouded, but its warmth was gone. With the girl, he felt a prickling along the spine. She turned her head slightly and, through her eyes, he saw, a few yards away in tall grass, a creeping man.

The eyes of the man were fixed on the girl's body and the traveler felt her thrill of terror. The man lay there for a moment, hands flat on the ground under his chest. Then he moved forward, inching toward her.

The girl screamed. Her terror gripped the visitor. He was helpless. His thoughts whirled into chaos, following hers.

The eyes of the creeping man flicked from side to side. The visitor quivered and cringed with the girl when she screamed again. As the torrent of frightened sound poured from her throat, the creeping man looked into her eyes. Instantly the visitor was sucked into his mind.

It was a maelstrom. A tremendous conflict was going on in it. One part of it was urging the body on in its fantastic crawl toward the young woman frozen in terror against the sky. The visitor was aware of the other part, submerged and struggling feebly, trying to get through with a message of reason. But it was handicapped. The visitor sensed these efforts being nullified by a crushing weight of shame.

The traveler fought against full identification with the deranged part of the mind. Nevertheless, he sought to understand it, as he had understood the other minds he'd visited. But there was nothing to understand. The creeping man had no plan. There was no reason for his action.

The visitor felt only a compulsion which said, "You must! You must!"

The visitor was frightened. And then he realized that he was less frightened than the man was. The terror felt by the creeping man was greater than the fear the visitor had experienced with the girl.

There were shouts and barking. He heard the shrill cry of a boy. "Go get him, Max!"

There was a squeal of brakes from the road and a pounding of heavy footsteps coming toward them.

With the man, the visitor rose up, confused, scared. A great shaggy weight hurled itself and a growling, sharp-toothed mouth sought a throat.

A voice yelled. "Don't shoot! The dog's got him!"

Then blackness.

"Mersey." The voice summoned the visitor, huddling in a corner of the deranged mind, fearing contamination.

The eyes opened, looked up at the ceiling of a barred cell.

"Dr. Cloyd is here to see you," the voice said.

The visitor felt the mind of his host seeking to close out the words and the world, to return to sheltering darkness.

There was a rattle of keys and the opening of an iron door.

The eyes opened as a hand shook the psychotic Mersey by the shoulder. The visitor sought escape, but the eyes avoided those of the other.

"Come with me, son," the doctor's voice said. "Don't be frightened. No one will hurt you. We'll have a talk."

Mersey shook off the hand on his shoulder.

"Drop dead," he muttered.

"That wouldn't help anything," the doctor said. "Come on, man."

Mersey sat up and, through his eyes, the traveler saw the doctor's legs. Were they legs or were they iron bars? The traveler cringed away from the mad thought.

A room with a desk, a chair, a couch, and sunlight through a window. Crawling sunlit snakes. The visitor shuddered. He sought the part of the mind that was clear, but he sought in vain. Only the whirling chaos and the distorted images remained now.

There was a pain in the throat and with Mersey he lifted a hand to it. Bandaged—gleaming teeth and a snarling animal's mouth— fear, despair and hatred. With the prisoner, he collapsed on the couch.

"Lie down, if you like," said Dr. Cloyd's voice. "Try to relax. Let me help you."

"Drop dead," Mercey replied automatically. The visitor felt the tenseness of the man, the unreasoning fear, and the resentment.

But as the man lay there, the traveler sensed a calming of the turbulence. There was an urgent rational thought. He concentrated and tried to help the man phrase it.

"The girl—is she all right? Did I . . . ?"

"She's all right." The doctor's voice was soothing. It pushed back the shadows a little. "She's perfectly all right."

The visitor sensed a dulled relief in Mersey's mind. The shadows still whirled, but they were less ominous. He suggested a question, exulted as Mersey attempted to phrase it: "Doctor, am I real bad off? Can . . . ?"

But still the shadows.

"We'll work together," said the doctor's voice. "You've been ill, but so have others. With your help, we can make you well."

The traveler made a tremendous effort. He urged Mersey to say: "I'll help, doctor. I want to find peace."

But then Mersey's voice went on: "I must find a new home. We need a new home. We can't stay where we are."

The traveler was shocked at the words. He hadn't intended them to come out that way. Somehow Mersey had voiced the underlying thoughts of his people. The traveler sought the doctor's reaction, but Mersey wouldn't look at him. The man's gaze was fixed on the ceiling above the couch.

"Of course," the doctor said. His words were false, the visitor realized; he was humoring the madman.

"We had so much, but now there is no future," Mersey said. The visitor tried to stop him. He would not be stopped. "We can't stay much longer. We'll die. We must find a new world. Maybe you can help us."

Dr. Cloyd spoke and there was no hint of surprise in his voice.

"I'll help you all I can. Would you care to tell me more about your world?"

Desperately, the visitor fought to control the flow of Mersey's words. He had opened the gate to the other world—how, he did not know—and all of his knowledge and memories now were Mersey's. But the traveler could not communicate with the disordered mind. He could only communicate through it, and then involuntarily. If he could escape the mind . . . but he could not escape. Mersey's eyes were fixed on the ceiling. He would not look at the doctor.

"A dying world," Mersey said. "It will live on after us, but we will die because we have finished. There's nothing more to do. The Change is upon us, and we must flee it or die. I have been sent here as a last hope, as an emissary to learn if this world is the answer. I have traveled among you and I have found good things. Your world is much like ours, physically, but it has not grown as fast or as far as ours, and we would be happy here, among you, if we could control."

The words from Mersey's throat had come falteringly at first, but now they were strong, although the tone was flat and expressionless. The words went on:

"But we can't control. I've tried and failed. At best we can co-exist, as observers and vicarious participants, but we must surrender choice. Is that to be our destiny—to live on, but to be denied all except contemplation—to live on as guests among you, accepting your ways and sharing them, but with no power to change them?"

The traveler shouted at Mersey's mind in soundless fury: "Shut up! Shut up!"

Mersey stopped talking.

"Go on," said the doctor softly. "This is very interesting."

"Shut up!" said the traveler voicelessly, yet with frantic urgency.

The madman was silent. His body was perfectly still, except for his calm breathing. The visitor gazed through his eyes in the only possible direction—up at the ceiling. He tried another command. "Look at the doctor."

With the glance, the visitor told himself, he would flee the crazy mind and enter the doctor's. There he would learn what the psychiatrist thought of his patient's strange soliloquy—whether he believed it, or any part of it.

He prayed that the doctor was evaluating it as the intricate raving of delusion.

Slowly, Mersey turned his head. Through his eyes, the visitor saw the faded green carpet, the doctor's dull-black shoes, his socks, the legs of his trousers. Mersey's glance hovered there, around the doctor's knees. The visitor forced it higher, past the belt around a tidy waist, along the buttons of the opened vest to the white collar, and finally to the kindly eyes behind gold-rimmed glasses.

Again he had commanded this human being and had been obeyed. The traveler braced himself for the leap from the tortured mind to the sane one.

But his gaze continued to be that of Mersey.

The gray eyes of the doctor were on his patient. Intelligence and kindness were in those eyes, but the visitor could read nothing else.

He was caught, a prisoner in a demented mind. He felt panic. This must be the mind-screen he'd been warned about.

"Look down," the visitor commanded Mersey. "Shut your eyes. Don't let him see me."

But Mersey continued to be held by the doctor's eyes. The visitor cowered back into the crazed mental tangle.

Gradually, then, his fear ebbed. There was more likelihood that Cloyd did not believe Mersey's words than that he did. The doctor treated hundreds of patients and surely many of them had delusions as fanciful as this one might seem.

The traveler's alarm simmered down until he was capable of appreciating the irony of the situation.

But at the same time, he thought with pain, "Is it our fate that of all the millions of creatures on this world, we can establish communication only through the insane?

And even then to have only imperfect control of the mind and, worse, to have it become a transmitter for our most secret thoughts?"

It was heartbreaking.

Dr. Cloyd broke the long silence. Pulling at his ear, he spoke calmly and matter-of-factly:

"Let me see if I understand your problem, Mersey. You believe yourself to be from another world, from which you have traveled, although not physically. Your world is not a material one, as far as its people are concerned. Your civilization is a mental one, which has been placed in danger. You must resettle your people, but this cannot be done here, on Earth, except in the minds of the mentally ill—and that would not be a satisfactory solution. Have I stated the case correctly?"

"Yes," Mersey's voice said over the traveler's mental protests. "Except that it is not a 'case,' as you call it. I am not Mersey. He is merely a vehicle for my thoughts. I am not here to be treated or cured, as the human Mersey is. I'm here with a life-or-death problem affecting an entire race, and I would not be talking to you except that, at the moment, I'm trapped and confused."

The madman was doing it again, the traveler thought helplessly—spilling out his knowledge, betraying him and his kind. Was there no way to muffle him?

"I must admit that I'm confused myself," Dr. Cloyd said. "Humor me for a moment while I think out loud. Let me consider this in my own framework, first, and then in yours, without labeling either one absolutely true or false.

"You see," the doctor went on, "this is a world of vitality. My world—Earth. Its people are strong. Their bodies are developed as well as their minds. There are some who are not so strong, and some whose minds have been injured. But for the most part, both the mind and the body are in balance. Each has its function, and they work together as a coordinated whole. My understanding of your world, on the other hand, is that it's in a stage of imbalance, where the physical has deteriorated almost to extinction and the mind has been nurtured in a hot-house atmosphere. Where, you might say, the mind has fed on the decay of the body."

"No," said Mersey, voicing the traveler's conviction. "You paint a highly distorted picture of our world."

"I theorize, of course," Dr. Cloyd said. "But it's a valid theory, based on intimate knowledge of my own world and what you've told me of yours."

"You make a basic error, I think," Mercey said, speaking for the unwilling visitor. "You assume that I have been able to make contact only with this deranged mind. That is wrong. I have shared the experience of many of you—a man, a boy, a woman about to bear a child. Even a cat. And with each of these, my mind has been perfectly attuned. I was able to share and enjoy their experiences, their pleasures, to love with them and to fear, although they had no knowledge of my presence.

"Only since I came to this poor mind have I failed to achieve true empathy. I have been shocked by his madness and I've tried to resist it, to help him overcome it. But I've failed and it apparently has imprisoned me. Whereas I was able to leave the minds of the others almost at will, with poor Mersey I'm trapped. I can't transfer to you, for instance, as I could normally from another. If there's a way out, I haven't found it. Have you a theory for this?"

In spite of his distress at these revelations, the traveler was intrigued, now that they had been voiced for him, and he was eager to hear Dr. Cloyd's interpretation of them.

The psychiatrist took a pipe out of his pocket, filled it, lighted it and puffed slowly on it until it was drawing well.

"Continuing to accept your postulate that you're not Mersey, but an alien inhabiting his mind," the doctor said finally, "I can enlarge on my theory without changing it in any basic way.

"Your world is not superior to ours, much as it may please you to believe that it is. Nature consists of a balance, and that balance must hold true whether in Sioux City, or Mars, or in the fourth dimension, or in your world, wherever that may be. Your world is out of balance. Evidently it has been going out of balance for some time.

"Your salvation lies not in further evolution in your world—since your way of evolving proved wrong, and may prove fatal—but in a change in course, back along the evolutionary path to a society which developed naturally, with the mind and the body in balance. That society is the one you have found here, in our world. You found it pleasant and attractive, you say, but that doesn't mean you're suited to it.

"Nature's harsh rules may have operated to let you observe a way of life here that you enjoy, but to exclude you otherwise—except from a mind that is not well. In nature's balance, it could be that the refuge on this world most closely resembling your needs is in the mind of the psychotic. One conclusion could be that your race is mentally ill—by our standards, if not by yours—and that the type of person here most closely approximating your way of life is one with a disordered mind."

Dr. Cloyd paused. Mersey had no immediate reply.

The traveler made use of the silence to consider this plausible, but frightening theory. To accept the theory would be to accept a destiny of madness here on this world, although the doctor had been kind enough to draw a distinction between madness in one dimension and a mere lack of natural balance in another.

Mersey again seized upon the traveler's mind and spoke its thoughts. But as he spoke, he voiced a conclusion which the traveler had not yet admitted even to himself.

"Then the answer is inescapable," Mersey said, his tone flat and unemotional. "It is theoretically possible for all of our people to migrate to this world and find refuge of a sort. But if we established ourselves in the minds of your normal people, we'd be without will. As mere observers, we'd become assimilated in time, and thus extinguished as a separate race. That, of course, we could not permit. And if we settled in the minds most suitable to receive us, we would be in the minds of those who by your standards are insane—whose destiny is controlled by the others. Here again we could permit no such fate.

"That alone would be enough to send me back to my people to report failure. But there is something more—something I don't think you will believe, for all your ability to synthesize acceptance of another viewpoint."

"And what is that?"

"First I must ask a question. In speaking to me now, do you still believe yourself to be addressing Mersey, your fellow human being, and humoring him in a delusion? Or do you think you are speaking through him to me, the inhabitant of another world who has borrowed his mind?"

The doctor smiled and took time to relight his pipe.

"Let me answer you in this way," he said. "If I were convinced that Mersey was merely harboring a delusion that he was inhabited by an alien being, I would accept that situation clinically. I would humor him, as you put it, in the hope that he'd be encouraged to talk freely and perhaps give me a clue to his delusion so I could help him lose it. I would speak to him—or to you, if that were his concept of himself—just as I am speaking now.

"On the other hand, if I were convinced by the many unusual nuances of our conversation that the mind I was addressing actually was that of an alien being—I would still talk to you as I am talking now."

The doctor smiled again. "I trust I have made my answer sufficiently unsatisfactory."

The visitor's reaction was spoken by Mersey. "On the contrary, you have unwittingly told me what I want to know. You'd want your answer to be satisfactory if you were speaking to Mersey, the lunatic. But because you'd take delight in disconcerting *me* by scoring a point—something you wouldn't do with a patient—you reveal acceptance of the fact that I am not Mersey. Your rules would not permit you to give him an unsatisfactory answer."

"Not quite," contradicted Dr. Cloyd, still smiling. "To Mersey, my patient, troubled by his delusion and using all his craft to persuade both of us of its reality, the unsatisfactory answer would be the satisfactory one."

Mersey's voice laughed. "Dr. Cloyd, I salute you. I will leave your world with a tremendous respect for you —and completely unsure of whether you believe in my existence."

"Thank you."

"I am leaving, you know," Mersey's voice said.

The traveler by now was resigned to letting the patient be his medium and speak his thoughts. Thus far, he had spoken them all truly, if somewhat excessively. The traveler thought he knew why, now, and expected Mersey to voice the reason for him very shortly. He did.

"I'm leaving because I must report failure and advise my people to look elsewhere for a new home. Part of the reason for that failure I haven't yet mentioned:

"Although it might appear that I, the visitor, am manipulating Mersey to speak the thoughts I wished to communicate, the facts are almost the opposite. My control over either Mersey's body or mind is practically nil.

"What you have been hearing and what you hear even now are the thoughts I am thinking—not necessarily the ones I want you to know. What has happened is this, if I may borrow your theory:

"My mind has invaded Mersey's, but his human vitality is too strong to permit him to be controlled by it. In fact, the reverse is true. His vitality is making use of my mind for its own good, and for the good of your human race. His own mind is damaged badly, but his healthy body has taken over and made use of my mind. It is using my mind to make it speak against its will—to speak the thoughts of an alien without subterfuge, as they actually exist in truth. Thus I am helplessly telling you all about myself and the intentions of my people.

"What is in operation in Mersey is the human body's instinct of self-preservation. It is utilizing my mind to warn you against that very mind. Do you see? That would be the case, too, if a million of us invaded a million minds like Mersey's. None of us could plot successfully against you, if that were our desire—which, of course, it is—because the babbling tongues we inherited along with the bodies would give us away."

The doctor no longer smiled. His expression was grave now.

"I don't know," he said. "Now I am not sure any longer. I'm not certain that I follow you—or whether I want to follow you. I think I'm a bit frightened."

"You needn't be. I'm going. I'll say good-by, in your custom, and thank you for the hospitality and pleasures your world has given me. And I suppose I must thank Mersey for the warning of doom he's unknowingly given my people, poor man. I hope you can help him."

"I'll try," said Dr. Cloyd, "though I must say you've complicated the diagnosis considerably."

"Good-by. I won't be back, I promise you."

"I believe you," said the doctor. "Good-by."

Mersey slumped back on the couch. He looked up at the ceiling, vacantly.

For a long time there was no sound in the room.

Then the doctor said: "Mersey."

There was no answer. The man continued to lie there motionless, breathing normally, looking at the ceiling.

"Mersey," said the doctor again. "How do you feel?"

The man turned his head. He looked at the doctor with hostility, then went back to his contemplation of the ceiling.

"Drop dead," he muttered.

the hoaxters

YOU GET yourself stuck off on a rock in space and after a while you begin to go nuts. Naturally. That's why Sam Black upset the chess board halfway through a game he certainly had not been losing to Alex Hurd.

"Sorry, Alex," he said immediately, looking disgusted with himself. He picked the pieces from the floor of the research station's dayroom.

"You've been out here too long," said Alex, putting the chessmen in their box.

"Yeah," Sam agreed. "It's not the company—it's the year between supply ships. We're compatible enough; our pre-tests ran enough alike for us to have been twins, almost. But I get damned tired of seeing nothing but your ugly face and those four laboratory walls."

"And the rolling pin," added Alex, whose pleasant face was long and high-boned, with a carefully tended mustache. "Rolling that hunk of steel over the rock specimens day after day. I've never really been convinced that it can't be done electrically, in a crusher. I think they want us to do it by hand so we'll earn our pay, maybe also to keep us too busy to think."

"It's the hand and the eye, Alex. The hand is slower than the eye, no matter what magicians say, and we could spot the particles. If we mashed everything up in a crusher, the stuff we're after would get sluiced away with the rock powder and we'd never see it."

"Assuming it's there to be seen."

"They wouldn't have sent us and our fat salaries out to this asteroid if there weren't a damn good possibility of finding the stuff. So I guess we'll just have to go on pounding."

"And sneezing at the dust," added Alex.

"And going nuts," said Sam.

Ninety-ninth Day

They weren't entirely alone on the asteroid. There was a native form of sub-life that the first explorers had discovered. But it was mostly dormant and didn't live on the surface. It consisted of slate-colored, unicellular hunks of stuff, as Alex described them, which moved around at point zero one miles per hour. They lived deep down in what either were natural tunnels or passageways they dug for themselves.

They seemed to live on something in the rock; it was possible that they dug the tunnels not so much to travel where it was they wanted to go as to get nourishment. The hunks of stuff—they were about the size of a thumbnail—were so close in color to the rocks they lived in, and on, that they were nearly invisible.

Sam and Alex had been told about them, that they were harmless, and had named them vizzies, for invisibles. They were as much company on their dull world as microbes on Earth.

"Check," said Alex Hurd. It was the inevitable chess game.

"You fell into the trap," said Sam Black, without enthusiasm. "Check yourself. I take the knight with my bishop and it's mate in two moves."

Alex studied the board and shrugged indifferently. "All right, you win. I'm getting careless. I'm tired. I want to go home. I want to see grass again, and trees. I hate rocks. I don't think we're doing anything important. I want to go back where the Sun comes up only once a day instead of every hour."

"Home is always nice when you're somewhere else," Sam said, his brown eyes far away. "But I wonder if it's home we miss as much as activity. If only something would happen here, the place wouldn't be so hard to take. But nothing ever happens. We crush rock. We test particles. We find nothing. We crush more rock. We

don't even know what they'll use the stuff for if we ever
find it.

"We send out the rocket. It takes pictures and beeps
its way around this dead old watermelon and the pictures
never show anything and the beep tone never discovers
anything we didn't know was there in the first place. If
only something would happen—*anything!* I don't give a
damn if it's good or bad, just so it happens."

Sam had put the chess pieces away and now he made
out their report to Base. The message went out once a
day—once every Earth day, that was; not every monoto-
nous time the oblong asteroid that was their temporary
world made a wobbly revolution on its axis.

Sam's leathery jaw tightened in distaste as he punched
out the daily report. It consisted of four words, which
hadn't varied in the three months, Earth reckoning, that
they'd been at the station.

The words were: "All well. Progress nil."

It was the "progress nil" which got them down as
much as any of the other things, such as their work being
so secret that they had no inkling of how their particular
research fitted into the Big Picture.

Their own work was the Little Picture, and it was a
serial movie with interminable chapters. It was at this
point in the dull drama that they began to wonder if
they'd ever see the final installment, or whether they'd
hand over their rock rollers to their successors at the
end of their hitch without ever having known what it
was all about.

"Progress nil." If they had anything at all to report, or
even if the wording were different so it didn't sound so
futile, their paid exile might have seemed less frustrating.

"Let me have the report," said Alex. "I'm going to do
something."

"What, for instance?"

"You'll see."

Alex took the blank. He crossed out the word "nil"
with an angry motion of his pen, scratched his mustache
reflectively, and then wrote busily for a minute. He
handed the sheet back to Sam.

"All well. Progress . . . Break for urgent. S.O.S. Research Station Nineteen. Attack on station by alien life-form from coordinates zero four eight x two seven. Request patrol craft blast spot as own armament ineffectual."

Sam read the message. "You're nuts," he said.

"I know it. Nuts from the monotony. Something's got to give and I don't want it to be me *or* you. We need a little excitement; you said so yourself."

"I was only talking. A gripe is a gripe, but sending out a false alarm—" He crumpled the message and tossed it away.

"Don't do that." Alex picked it up and smoothed it out. "We'll make it plausible. We'll blow up a couple of pieces of old junk near the station and send a few shells over. Set the stage, you know. The patrol will come and blast away and then the crew will come in and talk about it and we'll have a good story for them and they'll stick around a while and we'll have new faces for a change and—"

Sam got up and paced around the small room. His serious face was pulled into a frown.

"We can't do it, Alex. It wouldn't be right. They'd find out it was a fake and we'd be kicked out in disgrace. What kind of menace could we whip up that would fool them? Not that we're going to, but just for argument's sake." He grinned, his eyes lighting with interest for once. "At least we can talk about it. It's better than chess."

"Good man," said Alex. "Of course, we won't do it if you don't think we can get away with it, or," he added hurriedly, "if you don't think it's right, Sam. But here's the way it could be. We could make the menace a stray explorer ship from Jupiter. Got off course, say, and landed here, thinking this was one of the asteroids in its own protectorate, instead of Earth's or Mars'. Mistaken identity, see? We send a message telling them to get off. Maybe the message is a little hot under the collar and they take offense—sling a shot at us. We fire back. Then they start shooting in earnest. We send the S.O.S. The patrol ship sends out one of its oblivion bombs. The patrol can't see the target, but it has the coordinates we gave them, and, of course, after the explosion there's nothing left of the explorer from Jupiter."

"It stinks," Sam grunted in disgust. "If that's the way your mind works, no wonder you're such a dud at chess. Look, we've got to work with what we have. You can't queen a pawn till you get it in the back row. No pirate ships or interplanetary monsters or any such baloney. We'll use the vizzies. All of a sudden, see, they come up out of the ground. It's a periodic migration or something of the sort; you know, like the birds going South, only not so often. They stop being just little hunks of stuff and join up into a real, plausible menace. Get it?"

"Yeah," Alex replied, dazzled. "That's better than my idea any day."

Hundredth Day

They had sent out the fake distress signal, in a revised version, after twenty-four hours of preparation.

"I must be crazy," said Sam. "How did I ever let you talk me into this ridiculous situation? Let's cancel it—say we were drunk or delirious."

"We can't back out now, Sam." Alex's eyes were alive with excitement. "Look, here comes an answer now. We're in business."

Sam read it. "The patrol craft. Coming at full speed from—God, it's a long way off! I hope the vizzies don't get us first."

"That's the spirit!" cried Alex. "Put yourself in the frame of mind and we'll be all right. Just picture it—the vizzies massed in tight Z formation, eating everything in their path, moving inexorably in our direction, as if they scent and resent us. The suspense is terrible. Will the patrol craft get here in time? Will the oblivion bomb have any effect? Will the brave researchers survive the creeping horde or will help arrive too late and find only human bones picked clean? Or will the bones, too, be consumed? Isn't it terrific? I feel like a kid at a football game again."

"But you look like a mad scientist." Sam was smiling now, caught up in Alex's infectious enthusiasm. His broad face was aglow. "Maybe you *are* crazy."

"Sure I'm crazy. So are you. But it's only temporary. This'll put us back on keel and we'll be able to stand it again for a while."

"Wait a minute," Sam said. "We forgot something. If the vizzies were attacking, wouldn't we have the photo rocket out taking pictures? The investigators are going to want to see the films."

"You're right," agreed Alex. "And we will show them a film, only they won't see a thing—just the landscape under infra-red. The vizzies are invisible. Right? Well, they blend so well with the slate that no one could see them from that altitude. And I've faked some beeps on the electronic probe, so we're safe there, too."

Another message came from the patrol craft. It had streaked a vast distance since its last communication and was urging the men on the asteroid to hold on if they could.

Sam radioed back that time seemed to be favoring the defenders. They had lobbed a few shells, he said, but the old-fashioned explosives were having no effect. The vizzies were moving so slowly, however, that it would be several hours before they could reach the station. At Alex's suggestion, he explained that they were plotting the vizzies' position electronically and repeated the coordinates they had given earlier.

Half an hour later, the patrol craft hove into missile range, although not into sight, and advised that it was ready to launch a rocket with an oblivion-bomb warhead. The hoaxters on the asteroid corrected the coordinates to move the mythical horde a few yards nearer the research station; then they radioed that it was okay to fire.

The station shuddered and rocked on its deep foundations as the o-bomb exploded nearly twenty miles away. The plotters sent out the photo rocket to take pictures. It came back with a film that showed an o-bomb crater a quarter of a mile across and a collection of beep tones that recorded a lot of radioactivity, but no vizzies.

Soon afterward, the patrol craft streaked across the star-filled sky and radioed for permission to land.

"Break out the clean tablecloth!" said Alex. "Company's coming!"

Hundred and First Day

"Do you think they suspect anything?" asked Sam. "They turn up their noses at our accommodations, they bunk and eat in their own ship, they roam around the rock as thick as berrypickers and they ask more questions than a five-year-old."

"It's routine," said Alex unworriedly. "They have to make a report. Be thankful we don't have to. The skipper said we could have a copy of theirs to send on to Base. Have you run into any of the reporters? That's where we'll have to watch our step."

"I saw the press rocket land, but nobody's been around yet."

The buzzer sounded. A lean, tow-headed young man came in through the airlock, took off his gear and introduced himself as Kirsten of Galactic News.

"Gentlemen," he said, "I assume you are the outcasts. Two of the far-flung researchers of the Exploration and Assessment Commission. If you are, and you must be, I greet you cordially and invite you to share with me this precious bottle. I offer it in the knowledge that if I were you, and if I had been here three months, I'd have drunk up every drop I might have brought with me against the possibility of snake-bite—or, in this particular case, vizzie-bite. Do I hear anyone decline?"

"You hear nothing of the sort," said Alex. "What you hear is me getting three glasses. I'm Alex Hurd; this is Sam Black."

"Delighted, gentlemen," said Kirsten. "The beauty of vizzie-bite, as I understand it, is that the critter can't be seen with the naked eye and that you are therefore unable to be absolutely certain whether you have received the mortal sting. And so you go to the medicinal licker—I *beg* your pardon, locker—according to schedule, as a

precaution against the dread possibility of being a vizzie
victim. Am I correct?"

"Do you always talk this way?" asked Sam.

"I talk the way I write, and I am a feature writer,"
said Kirsten. "For the other fellow, the dross of cold fact,
the colorless statistic; for me, the delicate fabric of em-
broidery, the phrase which recreates the scene in vivid
life, the sentence which tugs at the heartstring and calls
forth the tear, or evokes the smile of true understanding."

"Yeah, you do that, all right," Alex admitted.

The reporter sat down and poured three drinks from
a half-full bottle.

"I have already been at it," said Kirsten, "as you will
observe. I drink; it is my curse and my sorrow. But it is
also my need and my joy. My editor often has said to
me, 'Randy, you are one of the few who give the press
corps a bad name. You are a lush, Randy, and your habit
undoes the good impression made by the majority of the
men of the press, who are sober men and faithful to their
wives. But you are a writer, Randy, who has a way with
words,' said my editor, 'and the way you have is such
that you would be snapped up instanter by the opposi-
tion if I fired you, and that is why I have refrained from
giving you the sack.' This is more or less what my editor
often has said to me, and I repeat it to you by way of
explanation should you think me unduly casual concern-
ing what conceivably was a marrow-chilling experience."

Sam and Alex left their drinks untasted as they listened
in admiration.

"This is as good as a floor show," said Alex.

"Better," said the reporter, unperturbed. "And there's
absolutely no charge. Now, would one of you be so good
as to describe your sensations for my stenographic ear?
I will take no notes, but the polished substance of what
you relate soon will be broadcast throughout the Solar
System."

Kirsten tilted his chair back and looked expectantly
from one to the other with his alert eyes.

They drank and talked. Alex carried the burden of the

conversation for the pair, although Sam occasionally put in a word of further explanation. He also gave Alex a kick once or twice when he thought his partner was embroidering the fabric of their yarn too much, instead of letting Kirsten devise his own ways to tug at the heartstring.

They had barely killed the bottle when other reporters arrived. They dropped their gear on the floor and took out pocket-size stenotypers. Alex repeated their story for the latecomers' benefit and some fresh bottles were opened up. At intervals, reporters went out to file stories, Kirsten among them. But they came back and, their work finished, settled down to have a party.

Crew members from the patrol ship joined the festivities in the researchers' dayroom, but the skipper remained aloof.

"Chess, anyone?" asked Alex, but it was a deck of cards he produced.

They played poker, drank, told stories and sang space ballads until the skipper came in to get Alex's and Sam's signatures on a statement and announce that his ship would be leaving in an hour.

The mission was completed. The skipper and the head of his investigation unit apparently were satisfied that the vizzie menace was ended.

The reporters had asked some astute questions, considering that they were laymen, but the plotters saw no hint of suspicion anywhere. They were jubilant. Their hoax had been a terrific success. They'd had their excitement. They'd had a lot of flattering attention. And they'd had a party.

Hundred and Forty-third Day

Alex said: "Let's have a party."

"What?" said Sam. He was trimming a beard he had started to grow six weeks earlier.

"A party," repeated Alex. "I'm getting bored again. I think it's time for another vizzie menace."

"Nothing doing."

"Aw, please, Sam."

"No." He snipped carefully at the short whiskers.

" 'No' or 'not yet'?" asked Alex.

"No," said Sam firmly. But then he added. "Well, not yet."

Hundred and Seventy-sixth Day

"You know," said Alex wistfully, "that was awfully good liquor Kirsten had."

"Who?" Sam's beard was quite full now. He combed it luxuriously.

"Kirsten, the reporter, that time we hoaxed them. Let's hoax them again, Sam. I could sure use some poker. I think if I play another game of chess, with you pulling away at that damn beaver you've worked up, I'll really go nuts. I feel like a pawn of fate, cast out into the void, left to be advanced one square at a time to my doom of ennui."

"Doom of what?" asked Sam, halting the comb.

"Ennui. Boredom."

"Just because you liked Kirsten's liquor, you don't have to start talking like him."

"I have a feeling I'm going to sound a lot worse pretty soon, if something doesn't happen. Then you'll be cooped up on this piece of nothing with a raving lunatic—maybe one with a beard phobia. You'll have to lock me up and roll all those rocks by yourself, and it'll take you twice as long to get no place with this damn fool research as it does now. Sam, let's have a party. Let's make the vizzies march."

Sam said: "Well . . ."

Hundred and Eightieth Day

The little spaceport on the asteroid was chockful of official craft. The patrol ship was there, an all-white vessel from World Government, two press ships this time, and a cumbersome-looking craft with cranes poking out of it.

The boys had cried wolf again, and this time they got more of a party than they had bargained for. The patrol ship had loosed another o-bomb. O-bombs were expensive. There was a second quarter-mile crater near the first and again there was no sign of a horde of vizzies. This was only natural, the hoaxters pointed out, because the o-bombs had obliterated them. But the skipper was not convinced.

Not this time.

He grilled Alex Hurd and Sam Black for two hours, then turned them over to his investigating officer, who grilled them some more. By then a World Government ship had arrived with a subcommissioner from the Exploration and Assessment Commission. The two researchers didn't dare back down now, and wearily they repeated their rehearsed story once more.

W. G. summoned an explorer ship and it came and poked its bores deep into the bowels of the asteroid. It lumbered here and there, as night and day chased themselves hourly around the tiny world, beeping electronically into the o-bomb craters, scooping up monstrous shovelfuls of slate and assaying them for signs of vizzies alive, vizzies dead, or vizzies disintegrated.

Then the reporters were allowed to see the two men. They came without liquor this time, but with broad grins and clever remarks. Sam and Alex squirmed through the interview. They stuck to their story, trying to pretend they didn't hear the cracks about the Moon hoax and the Cardiff giant, and repeating again and again their invented description of how the vizzies had attacked in Z formation, until they grew utterly sick of the ridiculous word vizzies—the reporters loved it—and their once-plausible story.

Kirsten was the worst of them. With his mock sympathy and his feigned seriousness, he almost trapped them a few times, but they wriggled out somehow.

The reporters finally left them alone and they collapsed on their bunks.

"Sam—" began Alex tentatively.

"Shut up," said Sam.

Kirsten dictated a story to Galactic News:

"By Randy Kirsten, Staff Correspondent.

"There is some doubt today whether a tiny creature of

primitive life, known to the trade as a vizzie (repeat vizzie, spelled v-i-double z-i-e), is as man-eating in its mealtime habits as two young scientists seem to fear. The native habitat of the vizzie is a forlorn asteroid somewhere beyond Mars which also is populated, temporarily, by the two young men.

"Their job is a secret one. It is also dull, and it was with great excitement that they fell heir to what they described as an imminent vizzie invasion of their own little half-acre nearly three months ago. The space patrol nipped that vizzie menace in the bud, according to the record, on which doubt has now been cast.

"But qesterday the alarm again went out from Asteroid X that the vizzies once more were on the march . . ."

And so on, from Kirsten, for three thousand words.

Hundred and Ninety-fifth Day

"We shouldn't have used that part about the Z formation," said Alex Hurd. "That's what sounded silliest of all."

"I've just succeeded in pushing the whole brainless stunt into my subconscious," Sam Black said. "I'll thank you to leave it there."

"I didn't bring up the subject. Base did. The message just arrived."

Sam took it. "Are we fired?"

"No. Just admonished. Pretty sarcastic, too, for an official document."

The message, from their chief, pointed out the cost of the two oblivion bombs, the cost of twice diverting a patrol ship from its normal course, the cost of sending an exploration vessel to a remote asteroid which previously had been explored to everyone's satisfaction, the personal cost to him, the chief, in aggravation, and the cost to the Commission in prestige as a result of the sly news stories which had appeared after the second "problematical" vizzie attack, as he termed it.

It must be assumed, he went on, that there really was danger, inasmuch as there was no proof to the contrary. This assumption, he said, must be the official version and, for its own sake, not theirs, the Commission must accept it and defend it whenever the matter might be referred to in the future.

But, the chief's message added, it was also true that there was no evidence to back up the researchers' story and he privately felt that the vizzie menace was a myth. Any subsequent deviation from routine without factual foundation, he warned, would be dealt with most harshly.

"File it," said Sam. "File it and remember it."

Two Hundred and Seventeenth Day

"The rocket's back," announced Sam.

"Let's skip it this time. Watching that film always puts me to sleep, anyway."

"Come on. It's got to be done."

They got into their spacesuits and went out to the landing rack to see how the rocket had made out this time.

"Missed again," said Alex. "I'll get the tractor."

He lumbered out to the rocket in the half-track and hauled it back. He took out the film pack and they went indoors to run it on the projector.

"Let it roll," said Alex. "I'm ready to hiss the villain."

The projector reeled off the routine circumnavigation of the asteroid as it would have appeared to a pilot if there had been one aboard the guided rocket. It was dull, as usual, watching the unending vista of gray slate—punctuated now by two o-bomb craters—and listening to the accompanying electronic beeps.

But then, as the film was ending, the beep device went crazy. It began to chatter, to whine. Then it keened up into inaudibility.

Alex, who had been curled in his seat, watching and listening automatically, shot upright.

"Creeping beepers!" he shouted. "What's that?"

Sam stopped the projector. Tensely, he spun it back a hundred feet and re-ran the film from there.

As the beep tone began to chatter again, the film showed a flat plain which they recognized as being some miles west of them on the simulated compass. There was nothing visible on the plain—not from the height at which the photo rocket had taken the pictures—but the chatter became a whine as the flat land sped by.

The beep tone began keening as the craft sped toward a sheer cliff. The cliff was the edge of a plateau atop which the research station was built. The beep device went into its silence of supersound just before the rocket passed over the cliff. The normal beep tone then returned and continued until the landing, when the film ended.

A magnification of the film strip showed nothing. The ground which had been photographed was flat, rocky and devoid of even plant life.

Working backward, the men found that the beep tone started acting up at the point where the film showed a small crater, not one of those made by the o-bombs. The crater had showed up on previous films, but it never seemed to mean anything except possibly that a meteor had struck there long ago. That was what it still looked like.

"This is a job for Buster," Sam decided.

Buster was their mechanical brain. He wasn't very bright, as such brains went, because there was no point in exiling one of the super-brains to a remote research station at a time when they were in great demand by Earth and the other developed planets.

Buster was fed the film. He chewed on it for a while, getting it into its proper channel, swallowed it and then digested it to the accompaniment of clicks and burps.

"Buster sure is a sloppy eater," Alex said, trying to cover up a case of nerves. "I hope this does not give him indigestion."

After a while Buster disgorged the film, together with a printed strip of paper. Sam grabbed it and compared the symbols on it with some on a chart hanging from one of Buster's buttons.

"I'll be damned!"

"What is it, Sam?"

"It's impossible. It couldn't happen. Not to us."

"What, for God's sake?"

"Buster says—this isn't fair!—he says the vizzies are on the march."

Alex looked at his bearded partner without comprehension. "I don't get it. What makes him think so?"

"Buster doesn't think; he *knows*. You can work it back yourself. When those beeps turned into a whine, it meant something unusual. Even a kid knows that. Buster listened to the whine—or checked the impulses that caused the whine—and compared them with the impulses made by things we have records of. If he didn't know what they were, he would have said so. He didn't, which means he knows. He has a record of the impulse a vizzie causes when a beep hits it. And he says the whine was caused by a lot of vizzies, *on the surface*. The whine got worse—more vizzies. Then it got supersonic. More vizzies than could be recorded at the threshold of sound, obviously."

"It's impossible," Alex objected.

"That's what I said. But I was wrong."

"They're a hoax. They don't march. We made all that up. It was a gag!"

"Well," said Sam, "it's backfired on us."

Two Hundred and Eighteenth Day

They sent the rocket out again, switched to film and telecast so they would have a permanent record as well as an instantaneous picture of what was going on now. And they adjusted it for radar-telecast, now that they knew what they were looking for. One half of the screen showed them the scene under infra-red in the brief night —a desolate plain of cindery slate, ending at a cliff. Apparently nothing moved.

But there on the other half of the screen, glowing in a mass that stretched along the base of the cliff and for as far back as could be seen, was an undulating sea of vizzies.

"At least they're not in Z formation," Sam pointed out.

"Ha, ha," said Alex in a flat voice.

"Can you make out whether any of them are on the face of the cliff itself? Climbing up it?"

"Wait till the rocket circles again. No, I can't tell. Can you see anything, Sam?"

"Look! There goes a piece of the cliff. Crashing down as if—I'll bet that's it, Alex. They're eating away the base of the cliff. They can't go up it, so they're eating their way under it. Millions of them—*billions!*"

"Call the patrol ship," said Alex. "At the rate they're going, they'll be here in a couple of days. There won't be any more plateau and our station'll go crashing down just like the cliff."

"Take it easy," suggested Sam. "The patrol ship wouldn't be anxious to come see us a third time. Remember, we're the boys who cried wolf."

"Sure, but there's the wolf! This time it's for real."

"Real, yes," Sam told him. "But is it dangerous? We're still keyed up to that make-believe menace we created. I don't think we're being entirely logical about this situation."

"Okay. Ten minutes out for logic. I vote for calling the ship and an o-bomb and taking our chances with their ridicule. But maybe you can make me change my mind."

"This gives us a chance to get out of the doghouse. It couldn't be more perfect. If we can wrap up this situation ourselves, we'll be the fair-haired boys again, instead of a couple of rock-happy bats."

They dug into old records at the station. They measured the length and width of the vizzie horde and its depth. They found that the creatures were eating vertically into the surface of the plain as well as forward. They sent the photo-rocket out on a shuttle basis, set to both telecast and film. They peered at the video screen and examined the film. They satisfied themselves that the plateau, with its sheer cliffs, was a natural, if temporary, barrier to the horde. They computed the rate at which the plateau was being eaten away and found that they had a comfortable span of time in which to make preparations.

Night gave way to day.

From the old records they learned that the vizzies had

never been run through a laboratory. The early explorers had satisfied themselves that the creatures were subterranean dwellers and had sounded them out with old-fashioned oscilloscopes to get a few basic facts about them. Then, convinced that they were useless and harmless, they had ignored the vizzies. They hadn't even named them.

There were some reports that the creatures made an occasional pilgrimage to the surface—"I must have half-remembered that when I was concocting our yarn," said Sam—but the reports had been undocumented and were put down to legend. There was no official record of such a visitation having occurred.

Until now.

Alex attached a grapple to the pilotless rocket and sent it out to get some samples. They watched on the screen as the craft dipped low and scooped up a bucketful at the end of a cable. When these were fetched to them, the researchers cautiously transferred the vizzies, by remote-control handlers, to a huge copper tank. Their slate color showed up well against the bright copper and the men watched as the creatures boiled around in the bottom of it.

The short day of the asteroid waned. The fleeting dusk became night as successive tests showed that the tiny vizzies had no taste for copper, iron, steel, lead, zinc, or any other metal or alloy of metal. But when rock or slate was dropped into a container with the creatures, it was gobbled up in a twinkling.

"At the rate they eat," said Alex, "you'd think they'd have gorged their way clear through the asteroid by now."

"Unless," suggested Sam, "they have only a short feeding season—which is what this must be—and they spend the rest of the time back underground, digesting."

But this question was academic. The problem was how to stop the horde from crunching into the cliff face and causing avalanches which eventually would undermine their plateau-top research station. It wasn't only a question of keeping the vizzies from overrunning the place; they had to be kept from collapsing it from underneath.

The problem had answered itself, in part, the next time the unmanned rocket flew over the horde. Continuing rock falls had transformed the plateau edge from a sheer cliff to a slope—a slope the vizzies were capable of climbing. And up they were coming, clearly shown in the image on the radar screen.

Sam tugged thoughtfully at his beard and Alex chewed on the end of a mustache which had become scraggly, while they watched the vizzies glitter their eerie way to the summit.

"Look," said Alex, "couldn't we fence in the station with metal? It'd take a lot of fence but we could do it. Then, even if they ate around us, we'd still be standing on solid ground."

"If you're thinking of the cyclone fencing we have in the warehouse," Sam pointed out, "you're thinking the wrong think. Metal doesn't repel them; they just don't like the taste of it. And the holes in a cyclone fence are plenty big enough for them to crawl through to get to the rock on the other side. Then they'd eat the foundations right out from under us."

"Yeah," said Alex. "That's a fact."

He sat down and thought hard. He got up and ran the latest films from the rocket through the projector. As he studied them, worrying his mustache with his teeth, he brightened.

"Now I *have* got it!"

Alex snatched up a portable searchlight and his gear and dashed out into the airlock.

Sam hammered on the door, then clambered into his own gear and went out through the second airlock. He chased after Alex through the starry night.

"Wait, you crazy nut!" he yelled.

He caught up with Alex near the edge of the plateau. By now the vizzies had reached the top and were moving forward with barely perceptible speed.

Alex fingered the controls on his gravity belt and soared a dozen feet into the airless sky, then nudged himself forward until he was above the horde. He played his searchlight down on the vizzies, first at one angle, then another.

The creatures were brightly visible, now that the men were so close to them. They continued to move forward. Sam stepped back and shouted at Alex. His voice was tinny in the transmitter.

"Get down from there, you dope! What happens if you fall in?"

"You might have to play solo chess," Alex replied placidly. "But don't worry. I think I've got them licked. Are they still moving?"

"Hell, yes!" cried Sam. Involuntarily, he stepped back another couple of feet. "If anything, they're moving faster."

"Good," said Alex from up in the air. "Now we'll see."

He dipped into a shallow dive and landed neatly beside Sam.

"Watch," he said.

Alex squatted, only inches from the vanguard of the vizzie plague, and shone his torch directly at it.

The creatures were stopping!

Moreover, they were retreating as the powerful light continued to play directly on them from the front.

"Come on," said Alex. "That's the answer."

The men went back to their station and turned on all the lights, letting them shine through the broad glass windows on the slate surrounding the buildings. A battery of searchlights set low at strategic spots completed their defenses.

"It clicked all of a sudden," Alex said. "We're east of the horde and they moved so slowly it was hard to tell. But for a few minutes, when the Sun rose, it was shining directly in their eyes, so to speak. It stopped them—but only for as long as the Sun was on the horizon. After that, the shell of their backs gave them protection and they came on again.

"And remember when we had those test vizzies in the copper pot in the lab?" asked Alex. "You saw how they went boiling around in it. They not only don't like horizontal light—they can't stand it. The light above the pot reflected on them from the shiny copper inside at all angles. It was too much for them."

When the time came for the men to send their daily report, the vizzies were swarming outside the station. It was entirely surrounded, but the creatures kept well beyond the shining circle of light.

The message to Base consisted of only four words.

"All well. Progress nil."

Two Hundred and Nineteenth Day

"They don't like animal flesh or cloth or rubber, either," said Alex. "So even if my light hadn't stopped them, I'd have been perfectly safe among them, out there."

"You didn't know that until today, though," Sam objected. "What else do the tests show?"

"That's all so far, Sam. Except that I think they're cute. Have you had a good look at one close up?"

Alex had a vizzie in his palm. He held it out to Sam.

Sam shuddered. "Disgusting little thing," he said.

"It's wiggling like that because the light's in its little eyes."

"Just keep your little pet to yourself," advised Sam. "It looks like the thumbnail of a corpse. What the hell are you doing now?"

"Feeding it," said Alex, picking up a slate pebble. "Poor little thing's hungry."

In a series of wriggles, the creature made its way across the lines of Alex's palm to the pebble and wrapped itself around it. The pebble vanished. Alex put another bit of rock on the opposite side of his palm and the vizzie wriggled toward it. That, too, disappeared.

Sam watched the performance with an expression of revulsion. But the expression changed.

"Alex!" he yelled. "Look! It didn't eat all the pebble. See what's left?"

"Where?" Alex examined his palm frowningly. "I don't see anything."

"The light has to hit it just right, it's so tiny—just a speck!"

Alex saw it now, too. But he said: "What of it? My vizzie's a fastidious eater. Likes to leave a little something on the plate."

"Let me test it," said Sam. "Just on a hunch."

And, of course, that was it.

The appetite of a vizzie led them to what they had been looking for in the slate rock—the rock they'd pounded and rolled in vain for seven months. They'd been unable to see the rare earth because it was in so minute a ration to the rock itself.

"What dumb luck!" Sam exulted. "The stuff turns out to be the one part of the slate the vizzie doesn't like—an infinitesimal bit of mineral. So small we could have gone on pounding rock till Doomsday without seeing it. Think how many pounds of the stuff we must have sluiced away, never knowing it was there!"

"Sweet little vizzie." Alex scratched the back of the creature in his palm. "I'm going to get you a whole boulder to nibble on to your heart's content."

"It is kind of cute at that, isn't it?" remarked Sam. He grinned. "Do you know what this means, Alex? Do you get the whole picture?"

"Sure," said Alex solemnly. "It means we'll have to catch a whole mess of vizzies and feed them rock, and then gather up their leavings. And I was afraid I'd have to do it all by myself because I thought you'd become a vizziephobe."

"You blathering moron! It means that every bit of ground the vizzies have eaten their way across is already panned for us. The plain, the cliff, the plateau—even our front yard. All we have to do to get the mineral is go out and scoop it up."

"Well, sure," Alex said. "That's fine, of course. But that means no more crushing and picking rock, which means even more time to go batty."

"What's on your mind?" Sam asked suspiciously.

Alex looked wistful. "I wish we could have another party."

lonely road

THE HUM of the tires and the throb of the heater had made him sleepy. He realized that when the hum became a squeal. He had taken a sharp curve unconsciously, at full speed. Time for a coffee stop, he decided.

He had been driving half the night. Another twelve hours to go. He could do it without sleep, if he didn't doze himself into a ditch. Coffee every three hours would help.

The red neon sign said EAT and the smaller one below it said *Dan's Diner, Truckers Welcome*. But no trucks were parked there, and no cars. Maybe Dan's coffee wasn't so good. He'd have to take the chance. He stretched his cramped legs and breathed the good cold air, then went in and sat at the long blue counter.

No one came. He picked up a cardboard menu, though he knew what he was going to have. Coffee and a hamburger, and a piece of pineapple cheese pie if they had it. If not, then apple.

Still no one came. He rapped on the counter with the menu. Then he noticed that there was no fire under the grill and that no coffee was being kept hot.

He went behind the counter to a door that stood ajar.

Behind it was a little storeroom, empty. He tried another door at the end of the diner. A washroom, also empty. Where was Dan?

There was a coke machine—caffein was caffein—but he wanted something hot. He went behind the counter again, prepared to apologize if Dan appeared, and took down a vacuum tin of coffee. He put water in the bottom of a glass coffee maker.

The coffee, as he brewed it, was foul. But he drank it, washing down a cold sandwich he'd made from meat and

cheese in the refrigerator. He had a piece of pie—apple—
and drank a glass of water.

He computetd the cost of the meal. He meant to leave
the money on the counter but he had nothing smaller
than a five. Feeling guilty, he went to the cash register,
rang up $.65 and made change.

He'd eaten too fast and the food lay heavy in his stomach. He breathed several lungfuls of cold air, got in the
car and drove away fast, headlights stabbing through the
blackness.

He needed gas. The luminous needle was uncomfor-
tably close to the luminous *E*. Another dial told him it
was 2:15. He'd passed a filling station a while back. The
gas pumps had been lighted but the gas wasn't his brand.
Any brand would do now. He found a station whose
pumps were aglow and whose little office was lighted.
He honked.

No one came.

He couldn't risk going on to the next one. He got out
impatiently and went to the office. It was empty.

Where was everyone tonight? Now that he thought
about it, he hadn't passed any cars for some time, in either direction. He couldn't remember how long it had
been. Since dark? Nonsense. Still, he couldn't recall having dimmed his country beams for an oncoming car.

Then he remembered the sudden rain in the late afternoon which had darkened the sky and blurred his windshield. Other cars had turned on their headlights, he
recalled now, and so had he. But his windshield wipers
had refused to work and for a time he'd driven slowly,
unwilling to get out into the rain to fix them. He'd come
to a wide underpass then, pulled over and stopped. Shel-
tered from the downpour by the mass of concrete, he'd
got out of the car and given the wipers a push. They
immediately took up their click-click. They'd been stuck,
that was all.

He'd been standing for a moment, stretching, when he
noticed two pools of water near a catch basin. They'd
reminded him of his son, dead these seven years. Among

the last things he and Joan had bought for the boy were two fishbowls Bobby wanted for his experiment. He stared at the two pools in the underpass, thinking of the boy and of Joan waiting at home at the end of his drive. He got back in the car. He couldn't remember having seen another car after that.

Now, at the gas station, there was no response to his *Hallo*. He shrugged and went to the pumps. Self-service night, he thought.

He filled his tank and went back to the office. He took out the four singles he'd taken in change from the diner and looked for a place to leave them. There was no cash register here. Greasy papers, catalogs and small tools littered the top of a battered desk. He put the bills down in a clear spot and weighted them with a pair of pliers.

After he'd driven on for some minutes he became acutely aware of the fact that he'd seen no one else on the highway. It wasn't a U.S. highway, true, but it was a good state road, usually well-traveled.

Puzzled now and beginning to feel lonely, he switched on the radio. But button after button yielded only the static of dead air. That was strange. Ordinarily, even if he could get nothing else, he could bring in WWVA. The powerful station in Wheeling blanketed the eastern seaboard in the night hours, playing its hillbilly records and hawking its patent medicines and illustrated Bibles.

The luminous clock said 3:10. He switched off the radio and hummed to himself, nervously.

He came to the outskirts of a town. Street lights hung over the road and there was an occasional light in a house. Cars were parked along the curbs. He began to feel better.

A traffic light turned from green to amber as he approached it, then red. He stopped. A block ahead was what looked like an all-night drug store. The traffic light turned green and he went ahead in low and parked. It was a drug store and it was open.

He pushed through the door and rapped on the counter. He'd buy a pack of cigarettes, though he had plenty, and mention jovially to the night clerk that he'd begun to feel that he was all alone in the world. He'd tell him about the empty diner and the unattended gas station. The clerk might have an explanation.

No one answered his rap.

The store lay bright around him, a clutter of magazines, school supplies, candies, tobacco products, a soda fountain. He looked over the top of a frosted glass partition, back to where prescriptions were compounded. No one was there.

He hungered for someone; anyone.

There was a telephone booth he hadn't noticed before and he went to it with relief. He'd been getting himself into a state. The voice of the operator would snap him out of it. He dropped a dime in the slot, got a dial tone and dialed Operator. He would tell her about the empty drug store and ask if she thought the police should know about it. He'd wait till the police came, he'd say.

He heard the ringing at the other end. At the tenth ring he pulled on the hook, got his dime back, reinserted it and dialed Operator again. After ten more rings he was beginning to sweat.

He unfolded the door of the booth and dialed 411, for Information. There was no answer.

He dialed 211, for Long Distance. No answer.

He dialed 611, for Repair Service. No answer.

He dialed seven times at random. No answer.

He fled out of the booth and out of the store. He roared the car away from the curb and through the town until he was again on the highway. It was more normal to be alone on the road. But his hand shook as he lit a cigarette. The clock on the dashboard said 4:55.

At dawn he turned off the headlights and rubbed his caking eyelids. His back and neck ached. He would have to stop and sleep. When he woke up maybe it would have been all a dream.

He found a tourist court. There was no one in the first cabin, marked *Office*. He signed the book, Clarence R. Spruance, and put a five-dollar bill between its pages. He noticed that he had left his car where it would block the way for others. So, to avoid anything that would jeopardize a return to normal when he woke up, he parked the car carefully in front of the cabin he chose.

He let himself in, locked the door behind him, washed the grit from his eyes, undressed to his underwear, prayed on his knees for the first time since childhood, eased under the covers and slept immediately.

When he awoke it was daylight again—or still. He stretched and scratched the bristles on his face. He would need a shave.

Then he remembered, all at once and in complete detail. And he knew it was no dream.

But perhaps it had changed. Maybe it was all right again—the people back, the noise and bustle and other cars on the highway. If they were, he would accept them. As a sort of bargain with himself, he would ask no questions. He would pretend they'd never been away.

But when he looked he saw nothing, heard nothing.

He was tempted to go back to bed, to try to sleep again, to give it another chance. For a long time he stood in his bare feet, looking out dully. Then he went into the bathroom and shaved.

He drove slowly, looking for a place to have breakfast. He didn't see any immediately and he drove faster. Then with a little laugh, he crossed to the far left lane and acceleratetd to 65 miles an hour, then 70. He held steady at 70, hugging the left edge of the concrete, laughing as he roared blindly around curves, bracing himself inwardly for a sudden head-on crash. His heart pounded at each left-hand curve and he had to force himself to keep his foot on the accelerator and hold the needle at 70.

But after a while he was taking the curves without panic and it began to seem normal to drive on the left. He felt depressed again, after his momentary exhilaration, and let the car decelerate to 40 as he eased across the road to the right.

He drove till he came to a gas station. He filled his tank, left some money in the office and drove on.

He noticed that he had only a few singles and some change remaining. There was really no reason for him to pay for anything but he felt that he must. If he did not, he would be accepting what was apparent—that he was the only person left. He would not accept that, and he determined that he would pay for what he took as long as he was able. It was a kind of insurance that the rest of humanity would return eventually from wherever it had gone.

So at the next town he went into a bank. At a teller's window he made out a check to cash, for two hundred dollars, signed Clarence R. Spruance, and pushed it under the grill. But there was no money within reach. He found his way to the back of the tellers' cages, went into the one he had picked from the other side and pulled open the drawer.

An alarm bell clanged, and continued to clang.

He stepped back in shock. Apparently there was a button that had to be touched so the drawer would open silently. The clanging unnerved him.

He made himself count out two hundred dollars, then count it again to be sure, and put the check in a slot where there were other checks. He shut the drawer but the harsh clanging continued. He made himself walk, not run, back around the cages and out the door. Another alarm was sounding outside with a terrible insistence.

The sound followed him through the empty town. He was glad to reach the open road again. He felt indignant about that alarm. It was unfair of it to have gone off that way, after he had been scrupulously ethical.

The tires hummed on the smooth road. The heater throbbed unnoticed. He didn't need the heater now, with the sun high and warm, but he'd neglected to turn it off. He became drowsy. His cigarette burned down and the heat of it on his knuckles roused him. He tossed out the butt and switched off the heater. Comfortable now but not sleepy, he drove for hours, automatically.

He slowed to read a sign. Forty-eight miles to go. As close as that.

He recognized the road now. The river was ahead, with a bridge. The toll bridge. He wondered if he'd be able to reach out and put a quarter on the counter inside the toll booth without leaving the car. He'd continue to pay as he went, people or no people.

He drove onto the bridge approach. You paid at the far end, he remembered. He slowed, took the quarter from his change pocket, transferred it to his left hand and coasted toward the booth.

A man in a gray uniform, with a badge, wearing a visored cap, stepped halfway out of the booth, hand extended, looking bored.

Spruance jammed on his brakes. The car bucked to a stop. The engine stalled. He sat, gripping the steering wheel, the quarter hard in his palm.

"Twenty-five cents, please," the uniformed man said.

Spruance held the coin out to him automatically.

"Twenty-five cents. Of course. That's right, isn't it?" He stared at the officer, felt the man's fingers pick the coin out of his palm. Stared at him. "You're back," he said.

"What?"

"I mean everything's the same. It's not—"

"Twenty-five cents," the officer said. "A quarter. That's what it's been as long as I can remember. You had it right."

"Yes, I did, didn't I? It's right, isn't it? It's all right again. The way it was before."

"Look, mister, you paid your toll. Now will you move along? Other people want to use the bridge, too, you know."

Spruance looked in his rear-view mirror. A car was behind him, waiting, and another car behind that one. Still other cars were moving along the highway at the end of the bridge.

The car behind him honked.

Spruance started his engine and went ahead slowly in first. The officer looked after him for a moment, then turned to take a coin from the next driver. Spruance shifted, then joined the road that ran south along the river bank. The car behind him made the same turn, honked again, then roared past. Other cars whizzed by from the opposite direction.

There was a sign, *POPULATED AREA*.

Then a town. A normal town, with people in it.

He found a parking space near a newsstand. He bought a metropolitan afternoon daily dated the 19th.

"Is this today's?" he asked the newsdealer.

"Yeah, sure."

He scanned the headlines but saw nothing unusual. He folded the paper under his arm and went into a lunchroom. Over coffee and scrambled eggs he looked at the paper from front to back, reading the first paragraph of each story. There was no hint in any of them that the major and minor crises of the world had been interrupted in any unusual way.

He beckoned to the counterman for a second cup of coffee. As he poured the cream in this time he noticed that it curdled slightly, as if it were a couple of days old.

"This cream isn't fresh," he said.

The counterman looked sullen. "I only work here," he said. "If you want to complain I'll get the manager."

"Never mind," Spruance said. He got up, leaving the second cup of coffee untouched. He put down some coins and left.

He went back to the newsstand. "You wouldn't have a copy of yesterday's paper, would you? For the 18th?"

The newsdealer mumbled, not looking at him: "No. Sorry."

"Well, does this town have a daily paper?"

"Yeah, but it's not out yet."

"I see. Where's its office?"

"Two blocks down, turn right half a block. But—" The newsdealer looked up at him, then down again, quickly.

"But what?"

"Nothing. Nothing."

Spruance thanked him and went on down the street. The people he passed either avoided his glance or looked at him with—hostility? That couldn't be right. It wasn't such a small town that a stranger would be noticed or resented. He paused in front of the five and ten cent store and pretended to look in the window. Several people passed, some in couples. He noticed that the hostility was general. Everyone was being distant with everyone else.

At the newspaper office he told the girl at the reception desk he'd like to look at some back issues.

"How far back?"

"Yesterday and the day before."

She looked troubled. "I'll have to call the morgue. The library, I mean."

"I know," he said, smiling.

She said into the phone: "That's right, the 17th and 18th. . . . Oh. . . . Okay, I'll tell him. . . . Yes, I know." She turned to Spruance again. "I'm sorry. They haven't been filed yet."

"That's all right. I'll look at loose copies."

"No, sir, you can't. We don't—we can't make an exception."

"I see." She seemed almost frightened, so he added: "It doesn't matter. Thank you anyway. Goodby."

It was beginning to get dark.

His wife answered the phone on the ninth ring. While it was ringing he'd had the lonely feeling again and had to look out of the booth to assure himself that the people were still back. So he spoke almost sharply to his wife when she answered.

"Where were you?" he asked.

"I was in the attic. How are you, Clare? Will you be home soon?"

"Yes. I'm in Hayesville. I'm all right, I guess. How do you feel, Joan?"

"Fine. Are you sure you're all right? How was your trip?"

"I'll tell you about it later. What were you doing in the attic?"

"I'll tell *you* later. It's a bit odd."

Joan had fixed coffee and a tray of sandwiches. "I thought we'd have a snack now and dinner later," she said. He nodded and kissed her absently.

"It's good to be back," he said. "I'm also glad you're back," he added with a little laugh. Then he told her what he meant.

She heard him out, frowning a little. "The check you left at the bank," she said. "That will come back in your statement."

"That's the only proof I have. If it proves anything. How about you? Are there two days you can't account for? Everybody I've spoken to seems to feel something's wrong but they won't talk about it. Will you?"

"I was in the attic when it happened," she said slowly. "I'd gone up to look at Bobby's aquarium."

Bobby, their son, had died when he was nine. They'd had no other children but kept the big house anyway, with its attic full of memories.

"The aquarium," he said. "Two of them, identical, for Bobby's experiment."

"There were two," Joan said. "There's only one now."

She'd gone up to the attic late in the afternoon. Bobby's things lay under the eaves, dim in the light of the naked electric bulb near the top of the stairs. The tricycle he'd outgrown. The two-wheeler he'd just learned to ride when he became ill. His stack of books. A first baseman's glove. The aquariums.

Bobby had been very good about his illness. He became a tropical fish enthusiast, spending hours watching the gaily-colored creatures dart among the water plants and in and out of the pottery castle in the sand at the bottom of the big tank.

Then one day Bobby had asked for another aquarium, exactly like the first, down to the last plant and the castle. They had bought it for him, of course, and set it beside the other near his bed. Bobby made adjustments in the slope of the sand, the angle of the castle and the spacing of the plants.

His mother wanted to know about the twin aquariums but he wouldn't tell her anything except that it was an experiment. Later, when she'd left the room, closing the door at his request, he'd transferred the fish from the old tank to the new one.

Bobby died not long after that. Later the fish died, too, and they'd emptied the two aquariums and put them in the attic.

"That afternoon," Joan said, "I picked up one of the aquariums and was holding it in both hands. I'd forgotten how heavy it was.

"Then I felt as if I was being *moved*. Not lifted or pushed—but *moved* in some positive way. The light flickered for an instant, then the feeling stopped. I was still holding the aquarium. I put it down. Everything seemed the same. Only it wasn't. There were *three* aquariums now."

"Three?" her husband asked softly.

"Yes. It was as if I'd been taken out of my own house—my world—and transferred to one that duplicated the old one down to the last smudge on the wallpaper. The way Bobby transferred the fish for his experiment. But they didn't fool me completely—just as the fish must have known their new aquarium was different."

"Who are 'they'?"

"I don't know. Whoever moved me and everybody else in the world—except you—to another tank, to study us for a while."

"And then transferred you back again?"

"Yes, this afternoon. I had the same feeling of being *moved*. I was here in the living room, dusting, wearing my yellow dust mitt. The feeling came and I recognized it. Then it passed and everything was familiar again. *Old* and familiar. I went to the broom closet to put the dust mitt away—and it was there already."

"You mean there were two dust mitts?"

"Yes. The one I'd been using—the duplicated one from the other world—and the one that had been in our own closet. So, after I thought about it for a while I went up to the attic."

He smiled. "To count the aquariums?"

"That's right. And there was only one. I'd taken one of them into that other world, and later I brought back an extra dust mitt."

"So they put you all in a new tank and studied you for a while and then brought you back. But why not me?"

"Yes," Joan said. "Why everybody *except* you?"

"Maybe I was overlooked, like the snail."

"The snail?"

"Yes. Remember how proud Bobby was after he'd transferred the fish to the new tank? He thought he'd done a thorough job till I pointed out that the snail was still in the old tank, hiding inside the castle. It was like me, fixing my windshield wiper in the underpass."

"Perhaps," his wife said. "I remember Bobby was annoyed because he'd missed the snail. But then he said: 'It was only an experiment. And not a very important one.' And, instead of putting the snail in the new tank too, he put all the fish back in the old tank. He said he thought they liked it better there."

love

HE WAS from Mars and she was from Earth; and you know what they thought of Martians in those days. He wasn't very tall, as Martians weren't; but that was all right, because she was unusually tiny and only came to his shoulder. They made fun of a Martian's anatomy then. There were a lot of jokes made by professional so-called comedians, just as it had once been considered funny to tell stories about Jews and Scotsmen.

Maybe Jac wasn't much to look at, by the standards of Earth model agencies, but he was intelligent and kind and Ellen loved him. She shouldn't have told her father that, she knew now. It had been difficult enough to be with Jac before the night she'd gone to her father with the confession of her love. He'd stormed up and down the living room of their house at the edge of the spaceport. He'd talked about position and family and biological impossibility. He'd invoked the memory of her dead mother and reminded her of the things he had sacrificed to give her the education *he'd* never had: the special schools and the tutoring. He said that if she could *see* this Martian—this Jac person—she'd understand his point of view and thank him for his efforts to spare her the anguish she would experience as a girl who had crossed the planet line. He didn't stop till he had brought tears to the blind eyes of his daughter.

Only then did he become calm and, with a faint twinge of conscience, tell her as gently as he could that she was not to see the boy again. He would see Jac, he told her, and explain to him that the thing was impossible.

Ellen felt her way to her room and locked the door

against him, and finally she heard her father go down the hall and slam his own door.

She refused to go down for breakfast the next morning. She waited till she heard her father leave the house to go to his job in the weather station of the spaceport. Then she left by the back way.

She heard the rattle of Pug's chain against the kennel and his bark of greeting. She knelt and took the paw he offered. It had been broken once and never properly set. She stroked it gently, although it no longer hurt him; it just made him limp. Ellen unhooked the chain from his collar and fastened a short leash to it. She and the dog went through the streets and into the Martian section of the town.

The whole community had been the Martian's originally. But after the coming of the Earth people they'd been gradually uprooted and forced into one end of town. Spidertown, she'd heard some people call it. Damn people like that, she thought. People like her father! "Damn them," she said aloud. And Pug growled in sympathy.

She bent down to pet him. He whimpered inquiringly. "Poor crippled Pug," she said. "A blind girl, a lame dog, and a Martian. Outcasts, Pug. That's us." Then she shrugged off her self-pity and walked on.

There was only one really bad crossing. It was a highway and the ore trucks rolled along it all day long, carrying their loads to the spaceport and the great Earthbound cargo ships. But the traffic man at the edge of the highway knew her and walked across with her and Pug.

"Beautiful morning, Miss Hanson," he said.

She said it smelled good and the air felt real fresh and thanked him.

Jac met her in the park at the edge of the lake. She tingled to the touch of his hand on her arm. His fingers were slender and quite bony and his arm, when he put hers in his, was thin. But he was strong, she knew: once he had picked her up and carried her across a rough patch of ground in the hills where they sometimes walked. He had carried her effortlessly, she remembered, and she had heard the strange rhythm of his heart as she leaned her head against his hard chest.

"Hello, Jac," she said, and Pug wagged his tail so furiously that it beat against her leg. Pug didn't care if Jac was a Martian, and she wished her father had as much judgment.

They went arm-in-arm across the park to the meadows beyond. Pug was unleashed now and frisked about them, his bark echoing flatly in the Martian air.

"This is a beautiful day—one should be so happy," Jac said. "And yet you look unhappy. Why?"

And so Ellen told him, and Jac was silent. For a long time they walked in silence until the ground began to rise and Ellen knew they were nearing the hills.

Jac said at last, "Your father is a good man and the things he wishes for you are things I cannot give you."

"If you're going to sound like my father," she told him, "I won't listen."

Then he was silent again for a time, but soon he began to speak seriously, and the gist of what he said was that she must forget him because he had been selfish about her. He said he had never really considered that there would be more to their life than just the two of them, and that they must not break her father's heart.

And she asked him, what about *her* heart? And his, too, he said.

And so they were silent again.

"Where are we?" she asked, after a while. They had been climbing for some time.

"I don't know," he said. "I have been thinking too much about us."

"Are we lost?"

"No," he said. "I can see the way we have come. But this is a part of the hills I don't know. You must be tired from the climb. We will rest."

They sat on the soft moss-covered ground amid some rocks and she leaned against his chest. Was he so different from Earth men? she wondered. It was so hard to know— for a blind person to know. If she could see Jac, would her father's warnings mean more to her? Or was her father merely intolerant of anyone who was different?

She had known so few men. Mostly, after childhood, her companions had been men who were kind to her for her father's sake. Many of them had been good fun and friendly, but none had ever been interested in her as a woman. Why should they waste their time with a blind girl? They hadn't, and Ellen had known no intimacy, no real happiness, until Jac.

But now she asked herself if she really loved him, as she maintained to her father, or whether she was grateful to him. What did she know of love? If she had once loved an Earth man, could she now love Jac?

It was so difficult. Her standards were confused. She did not even know what an Earth man looked like.

"Let me touch you, Jac," she said.

He gave her his hand and she seemed to feel his eyes on her face.

Her fingers traveled up his familiar arm, to his shoulder. The shoulder was bony and sharp, but so was hers. His neck was thick and his chin was not so well defined as her father's. Jac's nose was broader, too, and his eyes were sunk deep in his head. The head was hairless, not partially, like her father's, but completely. Ellen knew it was not usual for Earth men to be hairless, not men as young as Jac. Ellen put her hand against his chest. It was hard and rounded and there was that strange rhythm of his heartbeat. She took her hand away.

"How do I seem to you?" she asked.

If their races were so different, wouldn't he be repelled by her—by the thought of her body and his together in marriage?

"You are beautiful to me, Ellen," he said. "You are lovely."

She sighed.

"But this does not mean that *I* would seem attractive to *you*," he went on. "I must say to you truthfully that I believe Earth people are more appealing to Martians—from an esthetic point of view, if not a political one—than Martians are to Earth people. But," he added, "I believe a Martian retains his good physical attributes until death. He does not become fat, or senile, or ill. He doesn't wrinkle and sag as do some of your people. I think this is in favor of your happiness."

"I must seem cruel to you," Ellen said, "to be so questioning of our love."

"No," Jac said, "you have a special problem. You must really know me before you can be sure."

Would he look strange if I could see him? she thought. Would I be ashamed that he is bald and big-nosed and chinless? She used these descriptions in her thoughts deliberately to see if they bothered her. Would the rest of his body disgust me if I knew it? I know him to be intelligent and loving, brave and devoted, honest and good. But would these qualities have meant anything to me, if I had been able to see and I had discovered them in him?

There was no answer.

"Where's Pug?" she asked.

"I don't know. He went over a rise some time ago."

Ellen stood up. "Let's look for him. You must want to know where we are, anyhow."

They walked slowly in the direction the dog had gone. The way was rocky and the path seemed to become narrower. It grew chill as the sun became hidden by a cliff. They walked along the base of the cliff and soon a second cliff was on the other side and they were in a canyon.

Jac described it to her as they went.

Suddenly he touched her elbow and they stopped.

"Now I know where we are," he said. "I've never been here before, but I know from the stories I've heard."

"Where?"

"This is the Valley of the Stars. We have a legend that it was first found at night. And at the end of it is the Cave of Violet Light. It's a beautiful legend. The Cave was found long ago. Then the way to it became lost. That was many years ago, before my father's time. But it is just as *his* father described it. The walls of the Valley are carved with lifelike figures from our antiquity. Here, some of the carvings are down low and you can feel them."

He placed her fingers and she traced out figures of people.

"We do not know what period of our history they represent, but the figures are Martian. Here," he said, "is the carving of a very young child—and a woman." He led her fingers.

Hesitantly, her fingers explored the carvings while his hand rested reassuringly on her shoulder. "The figures are unclothed," she said.

"Yes."

The carvings were right to her touch and yet elusively, indefinitely wrong. Perhaps she could not judge the relative proportions. She could not tell. She became uneasy. "Why, it's only a baby—the child," she said.

"No," Jac said. "The child is three or four years old."

Her hand dropped.

Jac took her arm. "Come," he said, "we'll see if Pug went this way. Toward the Cave."

She walked in silence beside him.

"The Cave is the real source of the legend. The Cave of the Violet Light. They say it is magic. They say it has healing properties—the Violet Light, That whoever stands in its glow is made well. That the lame walk, and the deaf hear, and the—"

He stopped, and Ellen felt him looking at her.

"Yes?" she said. "And the blind?"

"And the blind see."

Jac continued, "It is a legend that linked with a time when we Martians ceased to become ill and to suffer the effects of age and deterioration. Our forefathers, so cured, bestowed the gift on all their descendants."

There was a barking in the Valley, echoing around a bend, and in a moment the dog was frisking toward them.

Ellen knelt and petted him.

"Hello, you Pug," she said. "Were you exploring? Were you in the Cave of the Violet Light?"

She could feel the dog's body moving as the tail wagged hugely.

"Were you?" she asked. "Were you in the Cave? Let me have your paw!"

The dog extended his paw to Ellen. She felt it.

"The other one!" she cried.

It, too, was whole. No bump or sign of a break any-where.

"Jac!" she cried. "Does he limp? Pug, I mean. Is he healed?"

"Silly girl. It's just a legend."

"Look at him!" she said. "Does he limp?"

"No. It is amazing, but he's well. Come here, Pug. Let me see your paw. The bad one. He *is* well, Ellen."

"Oh, Jac!"

"I have never really believed it possible—and never really disbelieved," he said slowly. "I suppose we Martians are less preoccupied with miraculous cures because we have so little need of them."

"But, Jac, it *must* be true!"

He took her hand, and they started down the Valley of the Stars in the direction of the Cave.

"Here is the bend," Jac said. "And there is the Cave."

"Describe it to me," she said. "Tell me how it looks."

"The entrance is like a triangle. As high as three men. There is rubble of fallen rock in front and a little way inside. And then it is clean and the floor is smooth, polished rock. And farther back there is a violet glow. It seems to come from the slanting walls, and the floor is like a deep pond."

"I've never seen in my life," Ellen said. "I was born sightless."

She felt herself trembling.

"I'm told violet is a beautiful color," she said. "Is it beautiful?"

"It is the most beautiful color I've seen. It's past description. It's so beautiful that you must be able to feel it if the light touches you."

Then he asked: "Will you go in?" His voice was hushed. It caressed her and soothed her and she stopped trembling. She loved him, now, the way she knew him. His thin hand was gentle and strong—holding hers.

The words leaped into her mind: Bald. Big-nosed. Chin-less. What did these words mean visually? What were ugliness and beauty to one who had never seen anything?

She remembered the figures her fingers had traced in the wall of the Valley of the Stars. The woman. The child—who was not a baby.

And she shivered.

Jac's hand tightened until her hand hurt. "You are afraid you will see me and find me ugly. In your mind they have made me something monstrous because I am different!"

"Let us go away," she said miserably. "I love you."

He was silent for a long while.

"If the Cave will let you see me," he said at last, "then you must. In the darkness, shadows become terrible things."

Her hand touched his face gently. He kissed the slim, cold fingers.

"Will you go in?"

"Yes," she whispered.

honor

WE ALL know the story of Serum M; once, the news was full of it almost exclusively. We know how Serum M rebuilds the tired cells—the ones that used to break down at the end of sixty or seventy years—and gives them the vitality to carry on for another score of years or more.

How many more we don't yet know. The life insurance companies probably will be the first to get the answer. Serum M has become a matter of hard dollars to them, and the lights are burning late in Hartford as their actuaries try to work the new longevity into proper relationship with their rate scales.

But very few people knew until Dr. Holsinger made his famous speech at the Nobel dinner what the "M" in Serum M stood for.

This is the way it was.

The research was done in a spare room of a weather-beaten old house near the spaceport on Mars. The house belonged to a man named Jac. Jac Mrlo or Mlro—one of those Martian names that no one knows how to pronounce. He's since become known as Jac Marlowe, or as one conservative newspaper decided it had to be, Mr. John Marlowe. But on Mars he was known as Jac; he lived in the house with his wife, Ellen, who'd come from Earth.

I say she'd "come from Earth" because when she married Jac she no longer was considered an Earth woman. Her father, a man of otherwise normal qualities, had virtually disowned Ellen when she and Jac married, and that was more than enough for the rest of the Earth colony on Mars. Jac and Ellen became outcasts—to the Earth peo-

ple, that is. The Martians had no such prejudices and
they welcomed the newlyweds to their community in
the Martian section of the Earth colony—a community
unfortunately referred to by the Earth people as Spidertown.

It made no difference to the Earth people that Jac was
a respected member of his own community. He was, in
fact, a research chemist, but no one outside Spidertown
had ever taken the trouble to find out anything more
about him than the fact that he was a Martian—one of
those short, skinny, big-nosed, hairless and nearly chin-
less Martians. The Earth people were job snobs, too; they
naturally assumed that Jac was one of those Martians who
hung around the spaceport doing the dirty jobs that no
Earth man could be hired to do. There are all kinds, in any
land.

Like most of the early colonists anywhere, the Earth
people on Mars presumed a superiority that did not entirely exist and dismissed the ancient culture of Mars as
possibly interesting anthropologically—but undoubtedly
of a low, almost savage, order.

That is why, when Jac Mrlo—not yet Mr. John Marlowe—ran his last test and was reasonably sure he'd got
the serum to behave the way he wanted it to, he became
discouraged. The excitement of the hunt had ended.
While it lasted it had been exhilarating; but now that it
was over and he had the prize it was no more than the
tail of a dead fox.

He explained it that way to Ellen, because, to please
her, he had been reading some books of hers about old
England, and the metaphor came first to his mind.

She was enthusiastic. But he knew that was her way,
and her wifely duty as well, and he discounted it. But
she talked and cajoled; and eventually he agreed that they
should take his serum and his carefully written paper to
the Earth people.

They decided that there would be slightly more chance
of success if she went, instead of him. So she went off
to the flight surgeon at the spaceport, who refused to see
her, and then to the health commissioner of the Earth

colony, who was frostily polite. The commissioner pretended to listen to her while he signed letters and initialed memoranda, and pleaded that he had too many official reports to read to take the time to read her husband's.

She was ushered out into the cold bright sunshine within five minutes, fighting to keep back the tears.

Ellen went next to her father. It was his day off from his job at the spaceport's weather station and he was glad to see her, in a regretful sort of way. But he let none of his happiness show and offered her tea, as he would any caller. He avoided all references to Jac and asked only after Pug, who was the dog she had taken with her when she left his home for Jac's. He didn't even mention the fact that she could see again after years of blindness because it had been Jac who restored her sight in some queer Martian way that he didn't care to know about.

She returned to Jac, defeated.

"What else did you expect?" he asked, his deepset eyes bitter in his hairless head. "We're outcasts, Ellen. I've always been one and you became one when you married me; it's something you've got to face, that's all."

"It's not fair," she said. "It's not fair."

"Of course it isn't fair," he said. "But that's the way it is, and you've got to learn to live with it."

"I won't," she said defiantly. "I'll live with you, but not *it*. They're fools, all of them, and they've got to learn."

"They'll never learn; that's the way they are. They only care about themselves, and what they can do. I knew that before you went. There's no use crying about their stupidity. I'll pour the serum into the sand, and burn the paper, and that will be the end of it."

"No!" she said. "You can't do that; at least use it for your own people."

"That would be like bringing sand to Mars," he said with a little smile. "Or, as in your books, coals to Newcastle. Our people have no need of a longevity serum. It's built into us; we outlive your kind three times over."

"Then you must give it to me," Ellen said.

"I would love to," Jac said, "if I were sure of it. But

I'm not. There is nothing so frightening to me as the thought that I might lose you. And the next most frightening thought is that you must die, by the nature of things, so many dozens of years before I do, even though I am already so much older than you."

"Then give it to me," she said again.

"No. I am as sure as I can be of my figures, my experiments with the Earth rodents—in my head. But I am not sure in my heart—and as long as you are in my heart I cannot do it."

"Then you must have it tested somehow," she said. "Otherwise I will think you don't care to have me with you for the rest of your life."

"You know that isn't true," he protested.

"Then you must prove it to me. I am a woman and I would die jealous of your next wife if I were old and senile while you were still in your prime. I am jealous now, in fact."

She assumed a quite serious expression.

"You must not be," he said, alarmed. "You have no reason to be. It is not logical—"

"*Women* are not logical," she said. "Maybe Martian women are, but Earth women aren't. So you've got to have your serum tested so you can give it to me. I shall nag you until you do."

"But how?" he asked. "Who would test it? You've been to everyone."

"Only here on Mars. I've talked to a very small—and narrow-minded—segment of a very small colony. The big men are on Earth. You must send it to—who is the leading geriatrician on Earth?"

"Dr. Holsinger, of course. Of Pan-Europe."

"He's the one. Send your serum and your paper to him."

"He doesn't know me," Jac protested. "I'm nobody. What's worse, I'm a Martian nobody."

"You are *not!*" said Ellen; "you're my husband. You pack the serum for space flight. I'll write the letter to Dr. Holsinger."

But Dr. Holsinger didn't reply.

As the months went by, Ellen became more and more furious, but Jac made excuses for his fellow scientist across the spacelanes on Earth.

"He's a terribly busy man," said Jac, "and a very important man. He must get hundreds of crank letters; you can't expect him to investigate all of them."

"I didn't write him a crank letter," Ellen said. "And no crank could have developed that serum you sent him."

"These things take time, even so," he said. "We must be patient."

They tried to be, for many more months.

Then, in one of the scientific journals Jac subscribed to, he read a disturbing paragraph. It was about a longevity injection the Klausens Institute was testing. That was Dr. Holsinger's institute. But nowhere was there any mention of Dr. Holsinger; certainly there was none of Jac.

"They've stolen it!" Ellen cried when she saw the paragraph.

"Nonsense," said Jac. "Many times different people have arrived at the same discovery by different methods."

"But not at the same institute!" she said. "That's stretching coincidence too far."

"We mustn't jump to conclusions," he cautioned, but his voice sounded hollow, and it was obvious that Ellen had already jumped.

The next news of the serum came not in a scientific journal but in the Earthcast.

They had tuned to the daily link with Earth and the staticky voice from the other world made a medical item the first on the news program.

"Dr. Ulrich Holsinger, the noted Pan-European scientist, today announced a new miracle drug which may banish the problem of old age," the voice said. "That is the gist of a report made public at the internationally known Klausens Institute. Dr. Holsinger's report was phrased in careful medical terms and he referred in it only to the patients who have been under treatment for the past sixteen months—but it seems clear that from the results in these cases the lifespan can be extended as much as a quarter century without loss of vigor or mental alertness. In other words, Dr. Holsinger seems to have licked the problem of senility in the same blow that has postponed death from old age. . ."

They listened, tense and bitter. Not once did the newscaster imply that the discovery was anyone's but Dr. Holsinger's.

When the far-off voice came to a transition that began "Meanwhile, on the political front," Ellen switched it off.

"Maybe," she said with a feeble laugh that trembled like the tears in her eyes, "when they've finished giving your serum to all the rich Earth people they'll let us *buy* some of it."

Later, Jac, behind his kindly-ugly face, tried to pretend that he didn't care. The main thing, he said in an over-casual voice, was that Earth had the serum; where it came from wasn't important.

Ellen told him quite frankly that he was a big liar; and she was equally frank in admitting that *she* cared a great deal personally. She didn't want to become a senile old crone until one day people mistook her husband for her son or her grandson.

Jac tried to laugh her out of it, reminding her that she was barely more than a teenager, but she refused to be consoled. It was more than just that, of course. It was the knowledge that once again the Martian's supposed inferiority had been thrown in his face. Earth would not admit that Mars could produce anything the Master Planet could not develop infinitely better. And Earth apparently had no compunctions about stealing from a Martian to perpetuate that myth. Even so respected a figure as Dr. Holsinger was tainted with Earth's intolerance and ruthlessness.

"I'm glad I left them," she said. "I don't want to be identified with a people like that."

They tried not to listen to later reports of the success with which the drug—it had now become known as Serum M—was being applied. But they could no more not listen than if it had been a child of theirs who had run away to find his fortune at the other side of space.

Finally the drug was taken out of the laboratory and

given to the pharmaceutical houses to mass produce. In its refined state it was rare and expensive to extract, and there were international debates about who should be the first to benefit from it—after the old people, who had been the human guinea pigs during its tests.

Some argued that the great statesmen of the world, many of whom already had outlived a normal lifespan, should be first; others thought the philosophers and scholars deserved it more. The philosophers themselves, replying to a survey by a news service, said the artistic geniuses of the world should benefit first—the painters, writers, poets and composers.

While the question was still being discussed, the Nobel prizes were announced and Dr. Holsinger was chosen to receive the award for medicine. He said he would give his views about who should benefit, at the time he made his acceptance speech later in the year at Oslo.

Ellen was furious. "The Nobel prize!" she cried. "They're going to give the Nobel prize to Holsinger for stealing your serum!"

But Jac by now was past anger. He merely smiled ruefully and wrinkled his big nose at her. "They are children," he said as if he had thought it all out. "Greedy children. Let them have their toys."

"You sound as if you'd given up," she said. "You mustn't do that. It just makes it easier for them. You've got to fight for your rights or they'll go on taking advantage of you—of us."

"I don't have time to fight just now," he said; "I'm too busy with something else."

It was true. He was off at the worktable in the corner, figuring something on a big sheet of paper, and it was likely that he'd soon be out in the lab, boiling things and pouring things into other things and watching things wiggle under a microscope. Anger is short; research is long, and infinitely more satisfying.

Ellen was drawn uncontrollably to the receiver for the Earthcast of the Nobel acceptance speeches. It was a special cast, carrying the ceremony in full, and Ellen resolved to sit through the whole thing. It was as if she thought her indignation and scorn would be communicated back across space to shame the Earth men as they spoke.

Jac pretended uninterest and there was the hissing of a gas burner and an occasional clatter of glass from the lab during the preliminaries to the ceremony. But as Dr. Holsinger was introduced, Jac drifted in; he sat his thin body down next to Ellen and his bony hand took hers.

Dr. Holsinger acknowledged the applause with a brief thank you. Then he departed from the tradition of the acceptance speeches and told a little story.

To most of his listeners, the story must have sounded strangely out of place. Dr. Holsinger talked about an ancestor of his, about a witch doctor in Africa and about a colleague he had never seen.

"A little more than a hundred years ago," he said, "a member of my family practised medicine in a city called Berlin. He was a good doctor, and at one time he had the respect of his patients and his colleagues and his community. But little by little this respect fell away. It was not because he had become a bad doctor or a poor one. He had not changed—the others had. You see, my ancestor was a Jew. And a hundred years ago, there was a great prejudice in the land . . ."

As Dr. Holsinger went on, the two people sitting by the receiver hundreds of thousands of miles away on another planet began to suspect that he might be talking to them. Ellen felt a prickling at the back of her scalp but sat very still for fear that if she moved, or even took a deep breath, something might happen to divert the speaker's train of thought and keep him from reaching the conclusion she was so desperately willing him to reach.

Jac gripped Ellen's hand very hard. But she dared not turn her head to look at him.

"Ten years ago," Dr. Holsinger went on, "a brilliant man went to London and studied medicine. Then, from medicine, he went into psychiatry. But then, instead of returning home, he set up practice in England. He was, as I said, a brilliant man—but he also was black. He was a

Bantu from Africa, and his father had the misfortune to be a medicine man in his tribe. And so the whispering began up and down Harley Street and eventually it ruined my psychiatrist friend. Who among the mentally disturbed would risk the gibes of his friends by going for treatment to a man the whispers said was a witch doctor? The Bantu went home in shame and I lost track of him. Perhaps he did become a witch doctor among those who respect the name. Whatever he did, psychiatry lost a great mind.

"Prejudice, my friends, is a fiendish, abominable thing . . ."

Ellen looked at Jac. "Oh, he is," she said. "He must be going to, now."

". . . two years ago," Dr. Holsinger was saying. "The parcel came from a far-off place and it was preceded by a letter. I studied the contents of both of them most carefully and I tested what was in the parcel. The tests took time, because I wanted to be sure.

"Then, prematurely, an announcement was made in my name. I had not authorized it, but it was out and I could not recall it. Nor could I at the time give the proper credit; the prejudice that eats at our vitality was still—*is* still, I fear—among us. I could not risk having the serum discredited because of it. The examples of my ancestor in Berlin and the Bantu in London came into my mind afresh.

"And so I was silent, and if my colleague in that far-off place is listening tonight I hope he will understand, finally, why I was silent, and forgive me. I accepted credit for what was not mine. But now the serum has been tested beyond all doubt; the world knows its worth and it can never be withdrawn. It is too late now for prejudice to go to work.

"Therefore tonight I most humbly accept your prize, but not for myself. I accept in the name of the discoverer of Serum M—Jac Mrlo, of Mars."

Dr. Holsinger pronounced the name exactly right, as if he had known it a long time.

The delegation of officials from the Earth colony had come to the little house in Spidertown, in an atmosphere that mixed gruffness, pride and embarrassment. One of them had made a speech, obviously prepared in advance. Then they had left, in a group, apparently glad to get away and have a bit more time to learn to live with this new situation.

Ellen closed the door behind them and then turned and looked proudly at her husband.

"They were kind of sweet, in their stupid way," she said.

"Huh," Jac said noncommittally.

"We will go to Earth, won't we?"

"No," he said; "I'm damned if I will."

It was the first time she'd heard him swear. "But why?" she asked. "It's all right now, isn't it? They've accepted us. That's what we wanted, wasn't it?"

"Maybe they have accepted us," he said; "but that doesn't mean we've accepted them."

"I don't understand. You're not going to be uppity now, are you, just when they've stopped?"

"That's not it at all," he said. "I'm just not going to be anybody's pet Martian."

"Pet Martian?"

"Don't you see, Ellen? It isn't good enough for them to accept me, just because I won a Nobel prize. I'm not better than any other Martian, and I won't let them make a big fuss over me to appease their consciences while they go on treating other Martians like dirt."

"Oh, Jac!" she said. "It's a beginning. There has to be a start someplace, and it just happens that you're it. You have to do your share. You owe them that much— and you owe Dr. Holsinger a great deal more."

In the end he went to Earth, of course. They gave him the VIP treatment all along the way and soon his skinny frame, his bald head, his shy-proud smile, his retreating chin and his big nose were known to everyone who looked at a newspaper or a video or a magazine. A few of the papers hastened to add a degree that was yet to be bestowed on him by referring in cutlines under his pictures to Dr. John Marlowe.

Looking back on the era now, from a historical vantage, we can see what a turning point it was in Earth-Mars relations. It was not only because of the way Jac Mrlo conducted himself—contemporary descriptions of this ranged from "impeccably" to the inevitable "credit to his race"—and the way the great of the Earth behaved, setting an example which in due course trickled down to everyday dealings between the people of the two planets.

These were important, of course. But there was a subtle and totally unexpected sort of poetic justice which developed from the widespread use of Serum M.

You see, the serum had its ironic side-effects, which some historians are inclined to believe did more than anything else to end the lingering prejudices of the Earth man against the Martian.

The serum prolonged life, true, and it arrested senility but it did nothing to halt some of the natural processes of aging in Earth men. Some even think it speeded them.

Thus the Earth men grew older and retained their vigor—but their hair fell out faster, their teeth deteriorated more than had been usual, their bodies slimmed down to a healthier size and their noses, which always had been growing anyway, grew still more.

It was a gradual thing, of course, and people didn't notice at first. But as the first crop of oldsters on Earth came into the new maturity induced by Serum M it became apparent that they—just like the Martians—were skinny, bald, big-nosed and chinless.

It got so that after a while it was hard to tell them apart.

88 beats 266

DR. LINDEN MARGATE, at thirty-eight, had not achieved the heights of fame he'd aspired to when he was attending medical school and so when the Planets Trust offered him the post at Venus Hospital he accepted eagerly, but without first consulting his wife.

Within two hours of the time he received the offer he had arranged with a fellow GP to take over his small midtown practice and packed the few things he wanted to take with him from his office.

There was a brief, intense quarrel with Gloria which changed the flushed excitement he had carried home with him to pale anger. She told him he was thoughtless and cruel and said she hated him and he said she was a selfish child—she was twenty-four—who was standing in the path of his progress. Then, when the heat of argument had passed, he spoke of the opportunities inherent in being the first resident doctor on Venus and of the five-figure contract and extra space pay and of how he would send for her within a year and how she would be the first woman on Venus.

She smiled then and made them both a drink and agreed that she had been unreasonable. This was his big chance, of course, and she mustn't interfere with his career. She understood that now, she told him, and she told herself how fine it would be to be the First Lady of Venus. She thought of it that way, in capital letters, and she thought also that this would be the path to riches and position which they had almost despaired of finding.

She kissed him soundly and a week later she stood behind the insulated observation dome at the 'port as a

slender silver needle with her husband **inside fough**t its
way through the atmosphere and out into space.

She stayed there watching until the fiery wake of the
ship was lost in the starry sky, and then went home
and tried not to sulk.

The year passed very quickly.

Gloria Margate was an attractive young woman. She
was blonde and tiny and pert. Her allotment check from
the Trust arrived promptly on the last day of each
month and it was generous enough to permit her to
complement her trim figure with an assortment of new
costumes and matching accessories.

Her sulks had not lasted long. The Margates had
many friends, and they had friends who had friends,
and a large number of these friends were men. At first
they were "safe" men, of conscience and principle, who
would not dream of making a pass at this temporary
widow who was so bravely bearing up under her husband's pioneering.

These escorts were succeeded by others who dreamed
quite intensively of making passes and by still others
who were not dreamers but men of action.

And so the months went by in a flurry of non-lone-
liness and sulkless evenings.

On one such evening a young man was interrupted
in her flat in the act of pouring cocktails for them by
the buzzing of the messagephone. He volunteered to
switch it on but his good breeding was such that he did
not read the message until her widened eyes beckoned
him to do so.

It bore a Venus dateline and said everything had
gone as planned and that the Margate apartment on the
hospital grounds was ready and aching for her. There
were details of the passage which had been booked
for her on the next ship. The message was signed
"LOVE LIND," and to Gloria it appeared to be in the
imperative.

And so she was defiant about it when the young man

suggested tactfully that the cocktail should be his night-cap.

She said there was no reason why their evening should be spoiled. It wasn't as if Lind were around the corner in, say, Africa, she said.

The young man thought privately that this was perhaps a crass way of putting it. But he thought more urgently that she was quite a gorgeous woman. And so he said lightly that the cocktails had got a bit warm and should be disposed of quickly while he made an icier batch.

They drank swiftly.

Gloria Margate boarded the spaceship with a rather bad conscience. But the hurtling, week-long voyage through the emptiness soon washed it to a light gray.

And so she was able to respond with genuine warmth when her husband kissed her passionately in the customs shed.

It was a dream of an apartment, air-conditioned throughout against the sultry mist of the Venus atmosphere but with thick non-openable windows that gave a romantic view of the lush grounds and the thin clouds scudding along incessantly at shoulder-level.

Linden Margate, M.D., had become a very important person on Venus. As Gloria, relaxing in an armchair, listened to him tell about it, it appeared that he occupied a place close to the top of Tier Two among VIPs. Tier One, of course, was unattainable, at present, for anyone not a member of the diplomatic corps. The diplomats just now were doing little more than the work of consuls. They kept their eyes on the doings of the Planets Trust, to see that it stayed within the bounds of its contract. But every so often they brushed up on their protocol and studied their instruction manuals in preparation for the day when human life might be found on the planet, or some suitably responsive intelligence.

Thus far not even an animal had been found, although there was a rumor among the botanists that the plant life would bear watching.

Lind had not been bashful about filling her in about his role on Venus in the past year. Gloria thought, in the first hours, that he perhaps had exaggerated his own importance, but that night at a reception in her honor at Planet House, she found that he had been modest indeed.

The Ambassador, a tall, erect widower, glowed for a moment in her exclusive presence at his side and told her that Dr. Margate was a first rate gem of a man whose treatment of the Ambassador's high blood pressure had been classical, downright classical, madam.

The Resident Director of the Planets Trust, grizzled and fatherly, shook his head in wonder at the emergency surgery Lind had performed on a workman mangled in the explosion of an ore-sample ship.

The Chief Botanist had never seen a man so calm under stress as Dr. Margate had been as he freed a researcher from the grip of a devil bush. Beautiful, nasty things they were, Mrs. Margate, which should only be admired in a laboratory from behind a screen. Gloria accepted an invitation to visit the lab.

The Medical Director saluted her beauty in scarce champagne, broken out in her honor. Any woman would be an asset to Venus, he told her, but to have Venus herself grace the planet was an unbelievable privilege. Gloria managed to blush under the compliment.

And that husband of hers, she was told—a man whose devotion to his wife was almost matched by his devotion to his work. Dr. Margate's research on growth under alien conditions, of both alien and terrestrial subjects, undoubtedly would be a very important contribution to medical knowledge.

Lind managed tactfully to steer his wife away from his boss and introduced her to the other VIPs, in descending order of importance. Gloria delighted in the attention and Lind beamed proudly.

Then there was music. An amateur band which had been practising for weeks struck up a waltz and Venus had its first ball. Lind was permitted the first dance, but none thereafter. The VIPs stood in line like schoolboys to take their turn at holding the planet's only woman in their arms for a few brief steps before the next one cut in to claim her.

It was quite late when the Ambassador stepped up to the bandstand. The lovely lady had had a long trip, he said, and they must not be selfish about her on this first night on Venus. They would have another party soon, certainly, now that Venus had ceased to be exclusively a man's world. Then with mock parliamentarianism, he proposed a vote of appreciation to Mrs. Margate for having made the occasion a glorious success.

There was a bantering amendment from the floor that it should be called "Gloria's success" and the assembled VIPs shouted approval.

Gloria, the success, and Lind, even more firmly entrenched among the VIPs in Tier Two, went happily home to bed.

Dr. Margate continued to be a very busy man, but Gloria managed to be even busier, although in a more decorative way. She was in high demand for functions where even the slightest reason could be manufactured for her presence. She dedicated new buildings in the expanding Earth colony. She became the official hostess at diplomatic-social affairs of Venus, whose frequency had tripled since her arrival. She was driven long distances through the mist to outposts where she delivered pep talks to workers and researchers. She was chosen "Miss Morale" and was presented with a giant bouquet of flame-colored, deactivated devil flowers.

Things couldn't have been more perfect for Gloria until one day she got two pieces of news with the force of a one-two knockout punch.

The first was that other women were on their way to Venus. She tried to console herself with the hope that they might be dull, unattractive and perhaps even middle-aged, but, whatever they were, she would no longer have the exclusive feminine concession on the planet.

The other was worse. Gloria, six weeks after her arrival, realized something she would not admit even to herself up to then. She was pregnant.

She told herself she was putting on a little weight, that was all. All those receptions and dinners, she told herself, those drinks and the rich food. She had busied herself with a needle to let out her clothes. And she took to wearing widely flaring skirts. They were dreadfully out of style—but then, as the only woman, she could dictate style, not be dictated to.

At seven weeks she was definitely alarmed. Her clothes were now all but impossible to wear. She felt nauseated. She'd felt that way often in the past few weeks, but she'd put that down to the climate and perhaps hangovers. Now she knew better.

She pulled off the constricting clothing and looked at herself in a full-length mirror. There was no doubt. But the shape she was in was not normal for a woman seven weeks pregnant. Gloria looked as if she was in her fifth month.

She sagged down to the floor, put her face in her hands and cried.

Dr. Margate was icily professional about it. He gave his wife a thorough examination in their bedroom, not looking into her eyes.

Finally he pushed aside the instrument kit and stood up. He looked at her and she returned his gaze helplessly.

She might have spared him this scandal, he said.

Scandal? she said. Was it a scandal to be a father?

He laughed mirthlessly. The fetus, he said, was late in its fifth month. There was a heartbeat. Was it true that five months ago they were on different planets?

She said nothing to that.

What would the Medical Director say? How would the Ambassador feel? How much longer did she think he would have his job if this became known?

She didn't know the answer to any of these questions. She moaned a little, not from pain.

He went on talking, for an hour. As he spoke, she felt that he was less outraged by the thought of his wife

having been unfaithful to him than by the discovery of
the fact of what this would do to his career. She had
thought she was greedy for attention and ambitious, but
now it appeared that the good Dr. Lind Margate was a
far bigger climber than she ever would be.

She would have to go home, he told her. Plead some
excuse—the climate, anything. Back at some Earth city
away from their friends she would have the baby. He
would not divorce her until it was born. Then he became
even more generous and said he would permit her to divorce him. She could charge desertion, easily, with him
on Venus. He looked morbidly pleased with himself for
being so noble.

He went out, walking as much as possible like a man
bearing up under great tragedy. He would be at the lab,
he said.

When he had gone, Gloria wondered why she had
been meek. Why had she let him be righteous simply
because her conscience was bad? She should have denied
everything, with as much righteous indignation as he
had mustered.

Sure she had been a naughty girl back on Earth.
But she'd been careful. Maybe her grandmother could
have made a mistake about such things in her day, but
now it was foolproof. There must be an explanation
other than the obvious one.

Her brows contracted. She tried, vainly, to remember
the date of her last sterility shot.

She remembered dimly that her hypo-needle had
broken and needed replacing. That had been the day she
picked up the silver-blue metallic costume from Madame
Fabriza. The lab was not far from her dressmaker.

She had replaced the needle; but did she have a
shot? If only her memory for dates were not so ap-
palling!

Her best bet, she finally decided, was to deny everything, to be the innocent, to let others believe her and
try to figure out an explanation. She was not going to
go back to Earth, that was for sure. Even with other
women coming to Venus, she'd be the dean of the

feminine corps. And she was reasonably certain she was prettier than any of her rivals-to-be.

She felt the baby flutter inside her. She lay back comfortably and crooned, as if to the child.

Everything was going to be all right.

Lind didn't come back that day and he was gone all night. He didn't call or send a message. Gloria began to worry. Maybe he'd been sincere about wanting to send her away. This, to her practical way of thinking, was very stupid; she was a definite asset to him here on Venus, no matter what. She wondered if her strategy of innocence, which she'd had no opportunity to test since she decided on it, would work. She thought gloomily how much better it would have been if Lind were a gullible business executive, say, instead of a physician with a strong background of obstetrics.

No, the innocence act was no good. She would try the forgiveness angle. She would work on his sympathy. She built up in her mind a situation which he could accept without too much loss of pride. She had been lonely on Earth without him. She missed him terribly. But once—just once—she had listened to some dear friends who said it would be good for her to go out for an evening and had arranged a foursome.

The man had seemed to be a gentleman. They'd had a few drinks at a night club and the man had taken her home. She felt a bit woozy. Not used to liquor any more, apparently. She remembered that he had helped her up the stairs to the flat, but that was all. The cad must have taken advantage of her. It was a terrible thing to have to confess and she'd thought she'd never have to, to spare his feelings, but now it had come out.

She went over the details a few more times and decided that it would do. Lind would accept her story. His ego would be hurt, but he'd get over that. And he'd have the satisfaction of forgiving her. It was a great blessing to forgive, she'd heard. He'd feel very noble.

The door opened. Lind came in.

His clothing was wet through, as if he'd been walking through the mist without his weather suit.

He had a strange look on his face.

He came and sat beside her on the bed.

Gloria started her story, but then stopped when she saw he wasn't listening.

He began talking, his expression dazed and his gestures vague, about rabbits and guinea pigs, chickens and bees, fruits and vegetables. It was crazy. At first.

He'd been working with them all along, he said. He should have known. He had the data in a dozen notebooks. It was all there and in his mind, too. Why hadn't he made the simple transference to human beings?

What was he talking about, she asked.

He was talking about her forgiving him, he said. For doubting her, he said. For having been cruel and horrible in her hour of trial, he said dramatically. For hurting the thing he loved most, he went on.

Gloria began to understand, dimly. She quickly dumped the story about the wooziness and the cad. She prepared to be just a bit cold, then to thaw, and finally to forgive. She would be generous.

Lind's studies in growth were the answer, of course. All the tests, all the experiments they had run pointed to the same conclusion. It was so simple, once you understood it.

Everything aged—grew—three times as fast on Venus as on Earth.

Everything from an eggplant to the Ambassador, himself. From a hen's egg to—to the baby his dear wife was carrying . . . Her baby—his baby. Theirs.

Human pregnancy on Venus lasted not nine months, but three. Eighty-eight days instead of 266. It was as simple at that.

What a cad he had been for doubting her. Could she ever forgive him?

She could—and finally did.

They became very happy.

And so when Clifford G. Margate, seven pounds, nine

ounces, was born three months from the date of Gloria's arrival on Venus, and after routine, impersonal blood tests had proclaimed him to be a true Margate, his father went before the Resident Board of the Planets Trust.

The board members listened skeptically, but then examined with mounting interest Lind's sheets of figures and statistics and lab reports on rates of growth and the way Venus accelerated aging processes.

Finally the Trust accepted, simultaneously, his arguments and his resignation and advanced funds to build a maternity hospital on Venus.

Under the arrangement Lind retained fifty-one per cent interest; the Trust soon found buyers for the other forty-nine per cent of the stock.

Construction of the Margate-Venus Hospital began immediately under priority AAA and, on Earth, the Margate Maternity Plan was launched with the biggest selective advertising campaign in recent history.

The slogan "88 beats 266" was the teaser. The appeal was to the rich women of Earth, those to whom, or to whose husbands, the cost of a round trip to Venus would not be prohibitive.

The not-quite-rich were offered All-Expenses-Paid Maternity tours.

"Why Wait 9 When 3 is Fine?" they were asked.

Having a Venus baby became the Thing to Do from Biarritz to Newport, from Palm Beach to The Riviera.

On the day Margate-Venus Hospital opened its doors it had reservations for a year in advance.

Venus boomed.

The Ambassador bestowed jointly on Dr. and Mrs. Linden Margate the Medal of Merit and the Margates were propelled forthwith into VIP Tier One.

The Ambassador then took the next spaceship back to Earth.

He felt he was getting along in years and even the lovely Gloria wasn't attraction enough to compensate for the fact that death was racing toward him three times as fast on Venus as back home.

don't fence me in

HAVE ANOTHER drink, Gyubi. *Woof!* I wish I had your double gullet, Pal—I'd use the lined one for pouring down this Venturan varnish of yours. If you ever get to Earth, Gyubi, you look me up. I'll buy you a real drink—something you'll want to pour down the gullet you taste with. As a matter of fact . . . but I'll get to that later. A story goes with it, as they say.

I was telling you about why we stopped building spaceships. The first one up from Earth crashed, you know. That was because when it reached The Barrier it tried to blast through it with its forward rockets. It got warned, then it went out of control. Crashed, all hands dead.

The second ship went up mad as hornets. Cautious, though. Cruised around, looking and listening. That's when they heard The Voice, the telepathic one that said nobody was to leave Earth until they said so.

The Federated Planets—we call it the Federation now —put it as tactful as they could but what they put was that us Earth people had a long way to go before we'd be worthy of traveling outside our own air. We had all those bad things they didn't want rubbing off on them. So Earth was proscribed. You know, nobody allowed in or out—especially out.

Well, you know how it is when somebody tells you you can't do something. Maybe you never cared particularly whether you did it or not, but the minute they tell you you can't, you want to, in the worst way. Like a thing we had once called Prohibition.

So we tried every way we knew to get a ship through the barrier. We tried mass breaks, hoping one of many would make it, maybe on an end run. But The Barrier was everywhere.

It wasn't a solid thing, that Barrier. It was like you were dropped into a life net. You'd go in a certain distance and it'd spring you back out. Hell of a sensation.

Along about that time somebody discovered invisibility, so we tried that. Sent up a spaceship disguised as an intercontinental rocket. It leveled off in a long cloudbank, then headed up. No go. It got bounced, too.

A bunch of amateurs at Woomera sent up a moon-rocket one day. An unmanned, remote-control, instrument-packed job. It got to the moon all right—through The Barrier—but nobody paid much attention. It landed nicely and sat there on the edge of Aristarchus sending back signals till the power ran out. But we knew all about the moon already and nobody wanted to go *there*. We wanted at the Federation.

Then the Asian bloc perfected telekinesis. The Anglo-Americans huffled around a bit, then ate humble pie and bought in. That was the Triple-A try—American ship, British skipper and takeoff from an Asian telekinetic field. It worked like all the others—a big flop. They aimed the thing at a point a hundred thousand miles past The Barrier. The ship disappeared from the field all right and everybody started slapping each other on the back. But a couple of minutes later there was the ship back again just where it started from, shivering a bit. The crew came out groggy, holding their heads. They didn't know what happened except they felt the same old sling shot effect of being bounced out of a net. And something extra this time. Every man-jack of them had a migraine headache that lasted a week.

Well, that was the end of it. We didn't try any more after that. We gave up. Licked.

Then how come I'm sitting here in a saloon on Ventura IV yarning about it? That's a fair question. Let's have another drink first, Gyubi, old pal, and then I'll tell you how I outsmarted you and your cronies in the Federation.

Yes, me, personally, all by my lonesome.

Well, after the Triple-A try got thrown for a loss, spaceships were a drug on the market. They put them in mothballs—saving face, you know, pretending they didn't exist. After a few years, when they got less sensitive, they put them up for sale. There weren't many takers but they were so cheap I bought one.

I was in intercontinental trade then. Telekinesis hadn't got started commercially yet. Those space jobs weren't what you'd call economical on fuel but when you converted them they held about three times as much cargo as an intercon. And they were so dirt-cheap I figured I could afford the upkeep.

I made out pretty good. Some companies shipped by me just for the prestige of having their dingbats and ducrots delivered by spaceship. But I always had the feeling the Federation was watching me as I baroomed back and forth across the Pacific, as if I was going to make another try at their blessed Barrier.

I always went solo. The pacer was so simple to handle I didn't need a co-pilot. And passengers were against regulations.

I'd delivered a dozen gross tons of flywheels, or mousetraps or corkscrews, I forget what, to Singapore and the customer tossed a big party which naturally I went to. It got late and I tried to ease off but when the host suggested one for the road I had to go along with it. He must have laced that one so it'd last all the way to California because when I set the autopilot for Muroc it was strictly a blind jab. Off we went, me and the spacer, *baroom*.

Well, that was it.

Next thing I knew I was out somewhere beyond Mars.

Scared the hell out of me when I came to, still boozy. The spacer was in free fall, headed clean out of the solar system, when the Federation ship came alongside. I pulled myself together as best I could. Drank a quart of milk, straightened my collar and prepared to receive boarders. Or get blasted to kingdom come.

But no. They were all kowtowy and if-you-please. I'd busted through their Barrier but they were too flamboozled to know it was an accident so they figured they were licked and offered terms. To me. As if I was the representative of Earth and this was all a carefully worked-out plan.

Of course I played along; I signed the compact that opened them up to trade. Me, an old intercon skipper, on behalf of Earth; but so hung over that only a lot of static filtered through to their mind readers.

That's all they were, Gyubi, you old barfly—mind readers and hypnotists. And that's all their barrier was, a vaudeville trick.

Sure I know you're not one of them, Gyubi. They're the robber barons and your people are the suckers, even if you are nominally members of the Federation. They had a nice racket—trade concessions on all twenty-seven inhabited planets this side of the Coal Sack—and they didn't want any of it lost to a smarter operator. That was us, on Earth, getting ready to take the giant step into space.

Naturally the Federation's mind readers didn't spot anything when I punched a leftover button on my control panel and put the ship into spacedrive. It was my finger did that, plus the one for the road; far as my mind knew, I was punching for Muroc, California.

Then by the time the spacer was headed up toward the stars it was too late. I'd passed out, and there just plain wasn't any mind for the mind readers to read or the hypnotists to toss the big Barrier whammy at.

Why am I telling you all this? Well, you figure it out, Gyubi. Why are you still exploited by the Federation? Because they can read your mind—outfinagle you every single time.

What you need, Pal, is an antidote. Happens I have a sample right here. Yes, sir—Singapore Sling, bottled in the full three-fifths quart size, only ten venturas the bottle. It goes right to work building a static field no hypnotist, no mind reader can penetrate. This is the equalizer, the way to be as big a man as they are.

You'll take a case? Smart boy, Gyubi. You won't regret it. Look at me—a living testimonial to the way this product works.

press conference

ONLY A few reporters were in the White House press room when the girl came in with the daily calling list. It was before nine o'clock on a frosty March morning. The girl thumbtacked the list to the cork-faced bulletin board, frowned at it, shrugged and then went back through the foyer to her desk in the Press Secretary's office.

The United Press man lifted himself, yawning, off the desktop where he had been sitting watching a news program on the television set at the far end of the room. He took a pencil and a fold of copy paper from his pocket and prepared to jot down the more interesting names, if any, from the typewritten list of those who would be calling on the President that day.

His yawn evaporated as he read the list.

It said:

CALLING LIST

10:15   Senator Jacob Javits, New York
10:30   Mr. Walter Reuther, A.F.L.-C.I.O.
11:00   Secretary of State
Noon   Budget Director
12:30   Lunch
 1:30   Mr. Kjal, Mars

Years of ingrained skepticism battled with the urge to spin into UP's private telephone booth and cry "Flash!" along the direct line to his office.

The skepticism won. He took down the list and studied that line

... 1:30 Mr. Kjal, Mars ...

The typist had been known to make some real boners in her day. Maybe she had meant to type Hjalmar somebody, as in Hjalmar Schacht, that one-time financial wizard of Hitler Germany. Or maybe it was Mars, Pennsylvania. There was a Mars in Pennsylvania, wasn't there? Or it could be a man from the Mars candy bar people—the ones who made Milky Ways. Better check.

He went into the Press Secretary's office.

"This 1:30 appointment of the President's," he said. "How about that?"

"What about it?" asked the Press Secretary.

The UP man put the calling list on the desk.

"This Mars business," he said. "Is that a typographical error?"

"No."

"That's a straight answer, anyway," the reporter said. "Now would you care to elaborate?"

"No," the Press Secretary said.

The UP man was exasperated. "Look," he said. "This could be the biggest story of the century, or it could be only as big as Aunt Emmy getting her foot caught in the screen door. Open up, will you?"

"You know I wouldn't give you anything exclusively," the Press Secretary said. "What you know from me the other boys have to know, too."

"I'm not asking for anything like that," the reporter said. "Just tell me this—or if you won't tell me, add it to the list, officially—when you say Mars do you mean Mars, Pennsylvania, or Mars the candy bar or Mars the planet?"

"I see your problem," the Press Secretary said. "Okay."

He took the list and inked in after Mars:

(The Planet.)

He handed the list back to the UP man.

"This is the straight goods?"

"The straight goods," said the Press Secretary.

"Is that all you'll say now?"

"That's all."

"Okay. Thanks."

The UP man went back to the press room, walking casually.

The Associated Press reporter looked up from the other end of the room as he entered and asked:

"The calling list out yet?"

"I've got it," the UP man said carelessly.

"Okay, after you," said the AP.

The UP said "Right" and eased into his phone booth. He lifted the receiver and whispered into the mouthpiece:

"Bulletin."

"Go ahead."

"Dateline. The White House indicated today that the age of interplanetary travel has dawned. Paragraph.

"The sensational disclosure was made in the most routine form possible. It appeared as a single line on the President's calling list, which is posted daily in the White House press room. The list shows the people who will call on the President in his office each day. Paragraph.

"Today it listed quote Mr. Kjal—K as in King, J as in Jerusalem, A as in Apple, L as in Liberty—comma Mars. (That's Mars the planet, Mac. Got it? Okay.) Unquote. The appointment was scheduled for 1:30 p.m.

"(Yeah, I know it's sensational. No, of course I'm not drunk. Yes, the Press Secretary confirmed it. Okay, make it a flash if you want to. Here's the rest. Hurry up, or the other guys'll get suspicious. Yes, it's a beat. You'll be two or three minutes ahead if you get it right out.)

"Paragraph. A reporter checked with the President's Press Secretary and was told that no mistake had been made in the list. At the reporter's request he confirmed that the Mars referred to was the planet Mars, and not a town or a company of that name. Paragraph.

"But the Press Secretary declined to elaborate. It was indicated that no further details would be available until the Martian had actually paid his call on the President. . . ."

The UP man came out of the booth, perspiring. He lighted a cigaret and tacked the calling list back on the bulletin board as the AP man strode over.

"You've been up to something," the AP man said. "I can tell."

"Yeah?"

"Yeah—say, what is this?" the AP yelled. He pulled the list off the board. His cry brought over at a run the third wire service reporter, the man from International News Service. The INS grabbed at the calling list but missed. The AP held it over his head and scowled up at it.

"Mr. Kjal, Mars," he read. "What the hell?"

The INS peered up, too. "For crying out loud," he said.

"It's on the level," the UP said. "You needn't go running inside. He won't tell you any more than's right there on the list. You'd better phone it in. I did."

The AP lunged into his booth and yanked the receiver off the hook. "You'd cut your grandmother's throat if your desk needed a good homicide," he said to the UP. "Bulletin!" he yelled into the telephone.

The INS threw himself into his booth and cried "Flash!"

The UP went back into his. "Send over two or three more guys," he said to his desk. "We may need them. For your information, AP and INS have just started dictating. AP's is a bulletin. INS is flashing it."

It was lunchtime, but no one went out to lunch. The White House press room was crammed with frustrated reporters who had learned there was nothing they could do until 1:30.

They had bombarded the Press Secretary with questions, which were met by a series of "No comments." The Appointments Secretary wasn't seeing anyone. The Department of State said all information would have to come from the White House. The Department of Defense said the same. The Federal Communications Commission said it didn't know anything and sounded sulky.

The reporters sat around smoking nervously or making themselves lunch from the stock of cold cuts and beer in their private refrigerator, or watching television.

The set had been tuned to a channel where a commentator was talking speculatively about the story while showing photographic slides of Mars and waiting for the arrival of his special guest, Mr. Robert Willey, the noted rocket expert.

The White House regulars were playing their complicated stud poker game, High Low Low-Hole Card Wild, but they played without enthusiasm and continually looked at their wrist watches.

One-thirty was H hour. At 1:15 they sent out scouts to watch all entrances to the White House, to see how Mr. Kjal would arrive and what he looked like.

But by 1:35 there had been no sign of him and by 1:45 the reporters were in a state of fidgets. Their desks kept the phones ringing to ask if the Martian had arrived and all the reporters could say was that they didn't know. The Press Secretary was no help. He declined even to say whether Mr. Kjal had reached the White House. The most he would do was to refuse to deny, when asked, that the visitor was a Martian from Mars. This negative scrap of information was duly passed on to the reporters' respective desks, who only demanded more, no matter how trivial.

At 2:15 the Cuban Ambassador, who had been standing, ignored by the press, next to the huge round table in the foyer, was shown into the President's office.

Mr. Kjal had not come out in the usual way, if he had ever gone in.

The Press Secretary leaned back in his swivel chair and declined to say whether the Martian had left by a side entrance. Was he still in the White House as a guest maybe? No comment. What were Mr. Kjal's plans? No comment. Would he describe the caller? No. Had he, personally, seen Mr. Kjal? No comment. It was infuriating.

Would there be a statement? Yes, one was being prepared now; patience, boys, please.

Finally the girl came in with a mimeographed statement. The copies were torn out of her hands and a torrent of reporters hurled themselves through the door, into the foyer where the Cuban Ambassador, hoping to be interviewed, was forced to jump to a sofa to avoid being trampled on. The reporters surged into the press room and to the telephones, yelling like wild animals.

On their way to the phones the reporters had discovered that the statement consisted of just one sentence. It said merely that the President and Mr. Kjal had had a 40-minute conversation during which topics of mutual interest were discussed.

The statement was dictated to their desks by the reporters with what elaboration they could muster, and then the torrent was back in the Press Secretary's office. There would be no further statement today, he said.

"The lid is on, boys," he said. That meant there would be no more news of any kind from the White House, short of something transcendental.

Would the President have a statement at his press conference tomorrow?

That would be up to the President, the Press Secretary said.

Would the conference be held at the usual time?

Yes, at 10:30 a.m., in Old State.

There the matter had to rest overnight. Thousands of words flowed out over the news wires and over the radio waves and through television receivers, but ninety-five per cent of them were speculation.

It was the biggest story since the discovery of the New World, but all the details could have been put into a thimble.

The auditorium in the Old State Department Building across from the White House was filled to the doors an hour before the scheduled time of the press conference. Every reporter with White House accreditation was there. So were scores of special correspondents for whom temporary cards had been issued and who had flown in from the north, south and west.

The three wire service correspondents were down front, in the first row of chairs. Close by were the men from *The New York Times*, the *Washington Star*, the *Chicago Tribune*, Reuters of London, Agence France Presse, and Tass.

There was a murmur of talk and a creaking of the wooden chairs as the reporters waited, impatiently. Even the most blasé of them might have admitted a tense excitement.

They watched the door the President would come through. He was late. His aides already were at their places at the front of the auditorium. Finally the President came in, alone.

He was smiling, but it was a subdued smile. He exchanged greetings with the three wire service correspondents and a few other reporters he knew by name.

The President waited quietly for the last of the talk to die away in the large auditorium. He took out a handkerchief and patted his head. He put the handkerchief away in an inside pocket, then adjusted the double-breasted suit.

When it was quiet the President whispered to an aide and received a sheet of paper.

He said he had an announcement. There was a great rustle of paper as the reporters prepared to write down each word. Then, with a grin, the President announced the appointment of a new member of the Federal Reserve Board. There was a laugh, in which the President joined, and some of the reporters dutifully made notes.

The President handed the sheet of paper back to the aide and said that was all he had today. Were there any questions?

There was bedlam. The President smiled and shook his head and raised his arms to quiet the noise. He asked those who had questions to hold up their hands and said he would recognize them individually. He nodded first to the AP, who asked:

"Is it true, Mr. President, that you had a conference

yesterday with a Mr. Kjal, a resident of Mars, the planet?"

The President, following custom in declining to permit direct quotation of his remarks, said Yes, and a very pleasant conversation, too.

The UP asked what language the conversation had been conducted in.

English, the President replied. Mr. Kjal spoke the language excellently.

The National Broadcasting Company asked if the President would repeat that pronunciation of the Martian's name.

The President did, saying the *k* was silent and the *j* was like the *j* in the French Jacques or Jean.

The INS asked for a description of the visitor.

The President said Mr. Kjal had asked not to be described and he would respect his wishes.

The *Christian Science Monitor:* "Is Mr. Kjal the representative of one race or nation on Mars, and if so how many nations are there?"

Mr. Kjal was the representative of the only race on Mars, the President replied, saying Mr. Kjal had full authority from his government to conduct the conference with the President.

The *Washington Post:* "Are the Martians friendly? Not warlike, that is?"

The President chuckled and said that Mr. Kjal was quite friendly.

The *Chicago Tribune:* "What form of government does Mars have? I mean, is it for instance a socialistic welfare state form of government?"

The President replied that the form of government was rather complex and could not be conveniently tagged with any one of the terms used on Earth.

The *New York Times:* "By what means did the Martian arrive and is he still here on Earth?"

The President said he was not at liberty to describe Mr. Kjal's means of transportation and added that the Martian had returned to his planet.

The *New York Daily Mirror:* "Did he arrive by flying saucer?"

The President, amid laughter, replied that he could say flatly that Mr. Kjal had not arrived, or departed, by flying saucer. He added that he would entertain no further questions about the means of transportation.

Tass, the Soviet news agency: "Why did he choose the United States instead of the Soviet Union to visit? Not that it isn't possible that the Martian hasn't already visited that great country, long before he came to Washington."

No comment, said the President.

The *Atlanta Constitution:* "Mr. President, I wonder if you would care to tell us, in your own words, the reasons behind the Martian's visit and what the meaning of it is, as you see it?"

The President replied that the visit had been an extremely interesting experience and he was honored to have been chosen by Mr. Kjal from among the Chief Executives of many great nations on Earth for the conversation they had had. But the President added that he would prefer not to discuss the matter philosophically; only in a factual way.

The three wire service men were becoming restive. They did not want the story to become too complicated. It had to be dictated at top speed after the traditional race to the telephones when the press conference broke up, and they'd had just about enough to handle easily. They needed one or two more points cleared up first, though, and after a hurried conference among themselves the three shot up their hands simultaneously. The President recognized them in turn.

The AP: "Does the Martian plan another trip to Earth, and if so, when?"

Mr. Kjal did not plan to return, nor did any other Martian expect to make the trip, as far as he knew, the President replied.

The INS: "Did Mr. Kjal say whether there were any

other planets besides Mars and Earth that have intelligent life?"

The President said that was a very good question but he regretted that the subject had not come up in his conversation with Mr. Kjal.

The UP: "Does Mr. Kjal's visit perhaps mean that the United States is closer to achieving interplanetary travel than most people realize?"

No comment, the President said.

The UP: "Let me put it another way, then. Would you say that one of the results of the visit was to help pave the way for peaceful relations between Earth and Mars when we eventually achieve interplanetary travel?"

He would, the President said; definitely.

The senior wire service correspondent cut through a sudden clamor of other questions from behind him to cry:

"Thank you, Mr. President!"

As always, that was the signal that the conference had come to an end.

The three wire service men broke into a dead run for their telephones.

That was all the world ever learned officially about Mr. Kjal, the man from Mars. The newspapers, the broadcasters, the television stations and the magazines played the story, sensationally or factually, in accordance with their editorial policies. Many newspapers printed the transcript of the press conference in full, to show their readers exactly how the story had developed.

Dozens of "it was learned" or "sources close to the White House" stories appeared in print, but none was authoritative and no one outside the President's official family ever knew any more than the President had told the press that day.

It had been the truth, of course, as far as it went.

But the President had not told the reporters that the visit from Mr. Kjal had been a strangely spiritual experience. In fact, the President by revealing the exact nature of their encounter might have had his sanity

questioned. And yet the visit could not have been ignored. The press, and through it the world, had to be
told—but just so much.

That night, in the privacy of his study with his personal journal open on his desk, the President tried to reduce his experience to words. It was extremely difficult.

Mr. Kjal had materialized in this very room two nights
ago, in the most reassuring way possible. He had sent a
thought ahead of him, telling the President what he intended to do, and directed the President's eyes toward
the wing chair beside the fireplace. Then, as the President watched, the chair shimmered as if momentarily
obscured by haze and Mr. Kjal was sitting there smiling.

The President found himself smiling, too. It was the
friendliest imaginable kind of meeting—no fear or doubt
marred it and there they had talked, for four hours, like
two old friends.

Their talk had been of everything and nothing. They
spoke of the President's deep concern that the Earth
might again be torn by war despite the hopes of its people for lasting peace. They spoke of hunger and disease
and of personal insecurity. They spoke of childhood.

The President recalled a tranquil time when he had
fished in a country brook with a golden-haired collie
sitting tall beside him on the bank. And Mr. Kjal spoke
of his childhood, too, in such a familiar way that the
President felt that his visitor might have been a boy
from the next town when he had fished the brook and
that if he had gone upstream they might have met.

No, he could not have described the conversation to
the reporters. He had explained this to Mr. Kjal and the
Martian himself had suggested that he make an appearance in the President's executive office the next day so
he could say truthfully that Mr. Kjal had been a White
House caller in the accepted sense of the term.

The President, seeking the right words for his private
journal, recalled an article in which the dean of a divinity
school theorized that beings of other worlds might have
supernatural gifts—which would have explained, theolog-

ically, Mr. Kjal's mysterious journey from Mars. The supernatural had no need of space ships. But the public did, if it was to accept Mr. Kjal at all.

The President thought then of the growing public belief that travel to Mars and other worlds was to be possible. But what strange forms limited imaginations had assigned to these men from Mars! How far from the mark they had been.

They had visualized semi-monsters instead of semi-gods.

He doubted if the reporters would have swallowed that one without considerable carrying on.

And how could the President have replied to the question put to him by the reporter from the *Atlanta Constitution?*

He could have said that since Earth had directed its attention to Mars and the conquest of the space between the planets a need had arisen for mankind to be worthy of that conquest. That Mr. Kjal was the embodiment of that need. That the greedy, belligerent, precocious infant Earth was on the path to the stars—a path bordered with things of beauty and fragility. That only a well-adjusted, mature Earth could be permitted to travel that path, as a friendly, curious creature in a new world —a humble creature willing to be shown the way.

But not a destroyer. A destroyer would have to be destroyed.

The President could picture the headlines this would have evoked: "Earth Gets Martian Ultimatum!"

No, he had said enough to the reporters.

Now the details of the Martian's visit were beginning to blur in his mind, desperately as he tried to retain them. But he knew this—because of the visit he would be a wiser man and through the great power of his office the world would be a better place.

The President mused for a time longer and then he wrote in his journal. There didn't seem to be much to put down, now.

He wrote only this:

"Had a pleasant meeting with Mr. Kjal, of Mars. He

is a fine, sincere man who represents a learned, peaceful people. He has returned home and said he would not come again. We will see him again, one day, but only when our people have the knowledge to permit us to travel to his land.

"It is my fervent wish that when the time comes we will be as spiritually advanced as we are scientifically and that the people of our world will live peaceably and profitably in communion with the people of his world.

"Mr. Kjal thought that everything would work out all right."

it's cold outside

THEY'D FOUND a way to make it stop raining in the city
and he didn't like that. Oren had one of the few outdoor gardens remaining in Greater New York and he'd
had to hook up an irrigating system fed by hose from
a tap in his basement. While he was at it, he ran another
hose up to sprinklers above the windows of his ground-
floor study and arranged them so they could send a
shower of water against the panes from outside.

He turned the rain on hard so that water drummed
against the glass with the realistic sound of a downpour.
It was almost satisfying. The bright sunlight streaming
through the drops spoiled it, somewhat.

Oren had known people who'd missed more than the
rain. Some had bid good-by to the city proper and
moved to the suburbs, though they remained within
the boundaries of the City-State. Others had fled Outside.

But there were those who had wanted, or needed, the
benefits of the super-metropolis—and they compromised,
as Oren and his wife had.

They'd diverted the rain away from the cities because
it was mostly a waste to have it fall there. It was better
to shunt it over to where it could fill a reservoir or un-
parch a desert or put out a forest fire—provided these
places were on resources land belonging to one of the
City-States. All very laudable, Oren supposed, but it was
an interference with nature that he didn't care for. He
was a conservative, an anti-progress crank.

Actually, euphemisms aside, he knew he was an anti-
regimentarian. Had he been one outside his private
thoughts, though, he would have been considered an un-

desirable member of society. It wasn't illegal, yet, to question the Suggestions of the City-State Council. Thus far, the Suggestions lacked the force of law. They served, however, to establish customs which most citizens found it wise to follow if they cared to avoid harassment by the green-tunicked members of the Council Guard.

It was no more illegal to be an anti-regimentarian in Greater New York in 2009 than it had been to be a Jew in the early days of Hitler-Germany, a Communist in the latter days of the United States, or a Conciliationist during the States' Rights Wars—in which the victors became the City-States and the losers were banished Outside.

But obviously it was healthier to keep quiet and follow Council-decreed custom than to seek justice in the letter of the law.

Oren was just sitting there in the study, smoking, not really thinking consciously about any of this, when his wife came in. His body was cradled to the optimum relaxation point in the restochair, but he was nervous.

"Oh, you've got the rain on," Edith said. "That's nice. But the sun kind of spoils it."

"Yes, it does," Oren said. "Pull the blinds, will you, honey?"

She darkened the room and curled up into a resto next to his. "That is better," she said. "Makes it more cozy."

He lighted a cigaret for her and for a time they sat quietly while smoke rose to mingle with the shadows of the room.

"It is today, isn't it, Oren?" she said finally. "I haven't been able to concentrate on a thing. I've got that orchestration sitting on the piano—the one that the maestro wants by tomorrow—but I don't have the patience to finish it."

"It's just routine, isn't it? Nothing you couldn't knock out in a couple of hours, I should think."

"Yes, but I seem to be so jumpy," his wife said. "I

know I'm not supposed to be. It isn't Modern, and all that, but I am."

He laughed and reached out a hand to pat her flat waistline.

"Old skinny-tummy," he said. "It used to be that only the husbands went through waiting and smoking themselves into a frazzle. Now the female of the species knows what it's like, too. Relax," he said. He tried to give it the casual touch. "Our baby will be born at the proper moment, sanitary, strong and just as squally as the old-fashioned ones. The obby said he'd call immediately from the delivery lab and we'll probably see him tomorrow, when the little bugger's adjusted to things."

"The obby!" Edith said. "What a terrible expression. Dr. Morales is the best obstetrician in Greater New York and you call him an obby, as if he were some kind of gadget."

"Well, isn't he? I think I'm being very modern and enlightened about this whole impersonal business. Our first child is being born six miles away in an antiseptic laboratory while its mother and father sit smoking and discussing terminology. Nine months ago they got a droplet of goo from me and one from you and mixed them in a high-gear cocktail shaker and ever since it's been growing in a bowl of heat-controlled expando-mush on a shelf where they look at it every so frequently and see that it's not going sour and agitate it a bit so it won't think it's forgotten. If that doesn't entitle me to call Dr. Morales an obby I don't know what does."

"Really, Oren, you're terrible," she said. "You talk as if somebody put something over on you. After all, you're the one who wanted to do it this way. I was perfectly willing to go about it in the old-fashioned way. There's no law against it—not really. Just a Suggestion. And we could have moved Outside, if necessary. We'd have gotten along all right."

"We've been over this so many times, Edith," he said. He was being angry in his icy-calm way. "Let me enumerate the points for you. One—we're both Intellectuals, so called. You're a musician; I publish talking books. It just so happens that the seats of our culture—the only places we could make a living—are the city-states. We're not farmers or workers and we'd be of no use on the Outside.

"Point two—if we left Greater New York where would we go? Chicagoland? The Bay? Dixieton? One's as bad as the other—and besides none of them has a decent publishing house, even if you could write your music wherever you had a piano.

"Point three—although it would be socially unacceptable to have a natural baby here, it would be safe. You'd have the best facilities, even if you got lectured at while you used them. Who knows what would happen to you Outside?"

"I'm sure people survive natural pregnancy on the Outside just as they used to," Edith said. "I think you've listened to the Council so long that you're beginning to believe everything you're told. Next they'll be telling you what kind of books to publish, if they haven't already."

She had become angry herself, now, as she did when he assumed his superior-logic tone of voice. Instantly he was contrite. He realized that he had been sharp with her only because she had verbalized the dilemma he wanted to avoid having to recognize.

"I'm sorry, Edie," he said. "I'm all tense. This waiting around for someone else to have our baby for us has me on edge. And you're right about the Council. They sent us a Suggestion last week. Very logical thing it was, too, on the surface. They noted that some of the titles on our back list haven't been moving well lately. That's true enough. They rarely do. They're standards, though, and the sales are steady, if small. But the Council Suggested that we let them go out of print. In the interests of conservation, of course. It was just a Suggestion, mind you; we can take it or leave it."

"And if you leave it?"

"I don't know. I think it's just a feeler the Council is putting out, to see how far it can go. I suppose if enough publishers took it, instead of leaving it, the next step would be a Resolution, to bring the rest of us into line."

"What kind of titles are they Suggesting you drop?" Edie asked. "Simply to help save tape, of course."

"Oh, some works on politics and government, as you might expect, and some less likely—such as a whole list of titles by Haskell, the naturalist."

"You're resisting the Suggestion, I hope."

"I don't know," he said. "We're having a conference on it tomorrow. We did take one of their Suggestions, but that was strictly meritwise."

"Oh?"

"It wasn't exactly a Suggestion. It was a letter of recommendation sent along with a manuscript by a Dr. Stern, the head of the Health Department. We're taping his book. It's about his pet theory, but it's sound. You know, the one about the creativity of women. I told you about it."

"I don't remember," she said. "But I don't think I'll like it."

"It applies to you, though. Stern's theory is that for so many hundreds of centuries women had been conditioned to motherhood that as a group they had a block against other channels of creativity. Even the unmarried and childless couldn't break the pattern because they themselves were the products of motherhood. Theoretically, that would be why you're having such difficulty with your music."

"But my mother was deconditioned," she protested. "She was born naturally, but I grew up in a bowl of mush, as you call it, and I intend to break the pattern."

"It's a three-generation process, Stern thinks," Oren said. "Not that I agree with him necessarily, but if we had a daughter, and if she were an obby baby, she might be the first to break the pattern in our family— if she had any talent, of course."

"You and your Dr. Stern can have his theory. I intend to break the pattern myself," Edith said. "Provided I don't fall back into it by having a baby myself in the normal way. I'll write that symphony yet, you'll see."

"Now you're being inconsistent."

She smiled as she recognized the truth of his remark.
"All right," she said. "But that's my prerogative. They
haven't bred that out of us yet. I'm still a woman." She
became serious again. "And I guess that's why I don't
know whether I want to have another baby this way. It's
so impersonal, so cold—like going shopping. This way is
so easy; it saves so much time and makes everything so
simple. But do you appreciate the things you get the
easy way, or do things only become precious to you
when you've had to suffer to have them?"

"Now don't give me any of that martyr talk," Oren
said. "Were you any less precious to your mother because you were an obby baby?" He grinned. "As I recall, you were about the most spoiled creature in
existence until I snatched you from the bosom of your
family."

His joke failed to return the smile to her face.

"I'm worried about something else," she said. "Aside
from the psychological aspects of the thing. I mean, have
I deteriorated . . . as a woman? I don't want to be just
a brain and a talent, if I am that. I want to be interesting
in that other way, too—the way grandma was when
she was a girl."

He turned in his chair to look directly at her. "Believe me, Edie, you're interesting. Oh, yes. Believe me."

Then he leaned over and kissed her soundly on the
mouth.

"If you wish," he said, "I'll elaborate on that comment."

"Do that," she said.

But the elaboration had to wait. There was a musical
tone and a voice said:

"Dr. Morales calling Mr. and Mrs. Oren Donn."

"There he is," said Edith. "There he is!"

"Now calm down," her husband said. "Are you ready?
Would you like a drink or anything before we talk to
him?"

"No. Go ahead, answer him."

Oren spoke the words that opened the communications circuits of their home to the doctor's call.

"Donn Fourteen. Hello, Doctor, this is Oren Donn. Edith's here, too."

"Hello," said Dr. Morales. "Your son has been born."

"A son!" Oren cried. "Do you hear that, Edie? It's a boy!"

"That's wonderful," she said. "How does he look, Doctor?"

"Perfect," Dr. Morales said. "He's a lively little tike. Got good color, too. Not all red like these natural children. He's had his first cry and his first meal and now he's sleeping. You can see him tomorrow at—say fourteen hundred. Will that be convenient for you?"

"That'll be fine," Oren said. Edith nodded agreement. "I'd like to bring him a little present, if I may. A little gold wristband my father gave me when I was born. Sort of a family tradition, you know."

"I'm afraid that won't be possible, Mr. Donn," the doctor said. "You know the rules. No foreign matter must touch him except what the laboratory provides. That's why you were advised not to buy any clothing or bedding in advance. We have all the things the child needs right here. In six weeks, when you take him home, you can dress him in an Indian suit, if you wish, but until then you must abide by our rules."

"Of course, Doctor," Edith said. "We understand. Tomorrow at fourteen hundred, then."

"Right. Goodby."

"Goodby."

The double goodby switched off the communicator and a single musical tone signalled that the connection was closed.

"Well," said Oren, "there he is. Born and everything. How do you feel?"

"A little weak. Honestly," she said. "I feel as if something had happened to me physically, just now. A lightening of pressure, sort of, and yet a kind of frustration. I can't explain it, really."

"It's strange," Oren said. "I don't know how a natural father used to feel, after he'd been sweating it out in a hospital corridor, but I'm pretty excited. But what bothers me is that I had the same sort of feeling when the dealer called up last year to say that our new gyro was ready to be delivered."

"Funny," she said. "He won't really be ours for six weeks. And until then I won't even be able to hold him in my arms except half an hour a day. What is that horrible name they have for it?"

"Parent Acclimatization."

He took her hand and squeezed it. Then he got to his feet decisively.

"I'll get you a drink. A good stiff one. Then I want you to go in and finish that orchestration. We've got to snap out of this."

"All right," she said.

"And while you're working, I'll go out. I feel like taking a walk in the rain."

"But there isn't any rain," she said, "except just outside the window." She turned a switch and stopped the drumming of the water on the panes. "You are in a state, aren't you?"

He laughed. "I certainly am. All right, then, I'll fix us both a drink."

Later, when Edith had finished the orchestration, Oren asked:

"Shall we see what's on the triveo?"

"I don't care," she said. "If you like."

When television first went three-dimensional it was called tri-video, to distinguish it. In time this was shortened to triveo, first with a long *i*, then with a short one. And there were many, like Edith, who changed the word once more—to *trivia*.

There was always a discussion about the triveo before they switched it on. Sometimes weeks went by during which it lay silent and unseen. Probably it was the least-used piece of equipment in the house, a price it paid for its lack of intelligent programming.

Oren pushed a button on the panel attached to the arm of his restochair and a section of the living room wall became the front page of the daily gazette. He dialed for the triveo section.

"It says Jerry Hilarious is on," he said.

Edith squinted at the projected page. There was a flat shot of a man in evening clothes, with his eyes crossed and his tongue held grotesquely in a corner of his mouth.

"Looks more like a Jerry Gruesome," she said. "Who is he?"

"A comic, it says. It's his triveo premiere. He's made a big hit in the pleasurants, it also says."

"I'm glad we eat at home, then," she said, "where we don't have to have belly laughs with our roast beef."

"Let's try him," Oren said. "We can always turn him off."

"All right," she said. "But you never do. You hang on to the grim end of everything."

"You've got to give them a chance. We wouldn't have any talent at all if everybody was condemned sight unseen."

"Off with their heads!" said Edith cheerfully; and later, when Jerry Hilarious had made his debut, she asked: "You call this *talent?*"

The comedian was a short, skinny man who gave the appearance of brash boyishness, though he must have been well into his thirties. He had a crop of scarlet hair whose vividness resulted either from dye or the affinity of the triveo cameras for the primary colors.

Jerry Hilarious also had an amazingly plastic face which he contorted at will and a repertory of startling gestures made still more fantastic by his apparent ability to throw each limb out of joint.

One of the gestures, delivered as if from a pitcher's mound, sent his forefinger streaking out by triveo magic so it seemed to be only an inch from the viewer's nose. Then the outthrust arm and finger moved to the southwest and its owner's comic high-pitched voice would say to a stooge with the utmost scorn: "Aw, g'wan *outside!*"

The gesture and the gag line were used several times during the program and it was obvious that these had helped to win him a spot on the City-State Network. It also was obvious that a new catch phrase had been born and that the Donns could expect to hear it often from amateur comedians among their acquaintances.

Mark Olafson had to be careful now. He had to use the utmost caution while appearing to be casual. Moving by night, it hadn't been too hard to cross open country undetected into the town on the outskirts of the City-State. From there, by stages, he had traveled nearly to the west bank of the Hudson River.

At the bus terminal, Mark went to the men's room and, waiting for a moment when he was alone, quickly but carefully redusted his face with talcum to hide the redness of the skin that marked him as a man from Outside. That done, he rubbed the excess off his hands and adjusted his borrowed clothing.

It was the best in the village and it had been pooled from among various owners for his mission. The village's best was only a seedy approximation of the everyday clothing of those he was among now. He pulled a telltale burr from the pants leg, wiped the shoes, adjusted the hat and, taking a deep breath, walked out into the terminal.

Mark ignored the moving pavement as being too open to scrutiny, and too slow. He bought a ticket to Timesquare and found the right bus. There were plenty of empty seats and he chose one in the back next to a window and tried to sink into it inconspicuously.

He saw the bus driver look back in his direction and he averted his eyes quickly. The driver seemed to be staring at him, but finally turned back. A few more people got on. No one sat beside him, luckily. The driver started the engine, closed the doors and the bus moved out onto the ramp leading to the tunnel under the river.

Oren Donn was sitting in his temperature-controlled, windowless office trying to decide whether to use good old reliable Smithson, with his fine familiar voice, to read the new pot-boiling historical romance into the tapes, or to experiment with a new voice, when the reception screen announced a visitor.

Oren pushed the papers to a corner of his desk and got up to greet the caller. The name, Mark Olafson, sounded familiar but he couldn't quite place it. But the man's face and the handclasp he gave him brought it all back.

"Mark!" said Oren. "You old scoundrel! I haven't seen you since school."

"That's right," the visitor said. He looked around the quiet, efficient office and dropped into a heavy lounge chair. "Hope you don't mind; I'm about beat." He sighed. "Been traveling." He looked carefully at Oren.

"Make yourself at home," Oren said. "Brothers of the Oath don't stand on ceremony."

Mark Olafson laughed. "Remember that, do you? It's been a long time since that schoolboy binge. You were pretty crocked."

Oren pretended to look hurt. "Held my liquor as well as a certain other eighteen-year-old I could name."

"Good old Donnie," said Mark. "Does the oath still hold?" He was serious suddenly.

"Of course." Oren looked at his visitor's clothing. He saw the rubbed places in the cloth and the worn shoe-soles. "I don't have a lot of cash with me, but you're welcome to what I've got—and I'll be here tomorrow."

Mark grinned. "That's more than I can say. Thanks, Donnie, but it's not money I need. Principally I need a friend—someone I can trust—a brother."

"Just a minute." Oren lifted a section of his desk and pressed a button.

Mark jumped to his feet.

Oren looked surprised. "Just wiping the tape. Don't be alarmed. I start it up in the morning and record all conversations. It's just a business gimmick."

"Does it go anywhere else?" Mark asked.

"No. I have it for my convenience. Lots of people do. Helps you remember things, if you've got a memory like mine. Here, take the spool. There's nothing important on it today." He unhooked it and handed it to his visitor.

"I'm sorry," Mark said. He sank back into the chair. "I've got a case of nerves." He took out a handkerchief and wiped his face. Some of the talcum came off. "You see, I'm from Outside."

"Oh." Oren looked grave and drummed on the desktop with his fingers. "That's where you've been. Pretty grim, I imagine."

"Yes and no. It depends on what you're used to—and what you want. For instance, I'm used to not having much—but I want a great deal. Does that sound paradoxical?"

"Yes."

"It's not, really," said Mark. "I don't have time to go into it right now, but one day we'll have a yarn about it. In the meantime, old brother, what I need are clothes that will get me by without suspicion, some kind of cosmetic to cover up my ruddy outdoor face that'll stay put for more than half an hour, and your solemn promise not to say a word to anyone—not even your wife, if you've got one."

"I have. She's Edith Riordan Donn, the composer."

"So she's your wife? Well, congratulations. We hear her music out there, once in a while. 'The Storm that Wasn't,' for instance. Good subversive stuff."

Oren wasn't sure this was a joke. "Look, Mark," he said, "I'll help you all I can. I give you my word, which should be superfluous. I'll bring the clothes and the makeup and I won't say anything to anybody. But because I do have a family—there's my little boy, too—I don't want . . ."

"I understand," his visitor said. "Don't worry. I'm deeply grateful and I wish I didn't have to be so mysterious. But that in itself helps protect you. And I'd go a long way toward death to avoid involving you and your family. I mean that."

Oren felt a thrill of vicarious adventure, but it was short lived. "I believe you," he said. "Shall I bring the clothes and things tomorrow. Here?"

"If you will. It's a busy office building, with people coming and going all day. Better than my going to your house, or meeting you someplace else." Mark Olafson stood up. "Now I've got to run. I'm very grateful to you."

Oren waved away the gratitude. "Tell me," he said. "Do you think—? I mean if my family and I—"

Mark Olafson's glance was keen but impersonal as it swept up from Oren's good clothes to his pale, well-fed face and around the luxurious, gadgetted office.

"Somehow, Donnie," he said. "I don't think you'd like it out there."

Martin was a very good baby.

He never cried, never was any trouble. He was sent to them in an ambulance ("Delivery truck!" Oren called it) from the hospital. He arrived in a cage of glass called a Sleeprplay. It was to be his home till he outgrew it. The thing regulated the temperature to the baby's needs, kept out insects, bathed him with anti-germ beams and made him inaccessible to random pats, cuddles and chin-chucks.

There was also a switch they could have used to soundproof the cabinet if Martin had been too noisy. But even if he had been the worst wailer in the world they wouldn't have considered using it against him, they said, and wondered who would be so heartless.

But though they derided the glass box, they found it a useful improvement over the old-fashioned crib and play pen. And much more sanitary.

There was a Chango at one end of the gadget. Oren never quite lost his fear that it would swallow up his son whole one day. It was operated by plunging the baby into it up to his waist and holding him there. Then, behind the scenes, the old diaper was stripped off, the baby washed and oiled and a new, pinless diaper fastened to his loins. The whole operation took thirty-seven seconds and the manufacturers were looking for a safe short-cut which would reduce the time to half a minute flat. But they hadn't yet found anything to make the diaper itself obsolete.

Martin was so little trouble they sometimes forgot he was in the house. He ate without fuss and slept well and the glass box discouraged much playing.

So Edith had plenty of time for her music. She worked hard and, sometimes when the baby was asleep and the piano was making a great racket, she would soundproof the Sleeprplay so he wouldn't be disturbed.

But she was often discouraged in the evenings when Oren returned from work and soon he found it was better not to question her about her progress. Tonight he had tickets to a theater. It was a surprise for her—a dance act was going to use some of her old music.

She met him at the door and, before he could tell her about the tickets, she threw herself at him with a hug that almost tumbled him off his feet.

"What's up, Edie?" he asked. "Martin been doing something precocious?"

He sometimes was bitter about their son; about the machine-like way in which he was progressing, without mishap, through infancy. And he always called the baby Martin, never Marty or any pet name.

"Now you stop that," Edith told him. "This isn't about the baby at all; it's about me."

"All right, I'll be good," he said. He followed his wife into the studio.

She sat him down in a restochair, handed him a highball and went to the piano. "Now don't be too critical," she said. "This is just the theme, with a few embellishments."

She sat for a moment with her hands poised over the keyboard, and then began to play.

There were five majestic notes at the beginning. Edith wove them powerfully into a statement which spoke authoritatively of revelations to come. Her right hand was the harbinger of the calm future, her left the evoker of monumental discord, raging in the dying throes of the tortured present. There was strength in her playing and meaning in the music. It stirred him even on this first hearing.

There was a kinship here with Beethoven, he thought, in the feeling, and yet it would be unfair to make a comparison on any other basis. He had sense enough not to mention it.

She finished on a chord that echoed away in the big room, then picked up a pencil and made a change in the rough score propped on the stand beside her.

Oren's face was serious when Edith looked at him.

"Not so hot, was it?" she said.

"Edie," he said, "you couldn't be more wrong. It's tremendous. I'm impressed more than I can say. I'm an old duffer about music—all I know is what I like—but you tell me I have good taste in good stuff. This is good stuff, Edie. It's the real thing."

She went to sit next to him.

"Do you really think so? Don't give me any malarky, Oren—not about this. It's too important to me."

"Of course it is," he said. "And it's going to be important to a lot more people, I think. Did this all happen today?"

"Sort of. It all went together today. I've had the theme—those first five notes—going through my mind for a week or more. I'd feel them pounding through me when I was doing something altogether irrelevant—like dipping Marty into the Chango, or hydrating his formula—but they didn't come out until I sat down at the piano today. Then there they were. They just came out of my fingers. I didn't even write them down, at first; they were so much a part of me I knew I'd never lose them."

"That's wonderful," he said. Then he asked: "Where do you think it came from?"

"What do you mean? The music? I wrote it, of course."

"Of course you did. I mean, do you think it has anything to do with the Stern theory? The one about nonbabying helping women create? You're a generation ahead of his schedule, if there's anything to it."

"I think his theory is a lot of egotistical male nonsense," Edith said. "The only reason women haven't become great musicians or artists—or generals, for that matter—is that we never got a chance to show what we could do. Not till lately, anyhow. Remember, it's been less than a century since women were permitted to emerge from the cocoons that the men had spun for them."

Oren smiled but said nothing.

"My theory is that Dr. Stern is just a crackpot," Edith said. "It's a matter of environment and opportunity, that's all. Otherwise why did it take man so long to write his first novel from the time he spoke his first intelligible grunt as a caveman? I wrote that music myself, without any mystic help from a sublimated sex urge. And I'd have written it just as well if Marty had been born in me instead of in a laboratory."

"Good for you," he said. "Then we've got a reason for celebrating." He told her about the theater tickets. She was pleased and ran to dress.

The dance act wasn't good and Edith's music seemed to her to be badly played by the orchestra. But it was an evening out and Edith squeezed Oren's hand to reassure him.

They hadn't expected to see a movie, too, but the curtains parted after intermission and there it was, in Ultra-Dimension, Authenticolor and Tactilivity, presented as a public service by the Department of Information, Greater New York.

A breath of cooled, somewhat rancid air swept across the audience and the sound apparatus played a stylized theme borrowed from a Tin Pan Alley relic that Edith recognized as "Baby, It's Cold Outside." The title of the film, formed by blocks of ice, was, simply, *Outside.*

The movie purported to be a travelog but they recognized it as propaganda. Nevertheless, after two reels of cineramic proximity to the gaunt, sullen-looking people who had chosen to live beyond the blessings of the City-

States, they decided they were extremely fortunate to be living where they were.

Oren, in addition, had the recent memory of Mark Olafson. His caller, who had been so nervous, so suspicious in the office, might easily have been one of the people in the film.

"That's not for me," Oren said later. "That's going back two hundred years—going Outside. Those shacks they live in—what did the commentator call them, quaint?—they're not quaint, they're primitive."

"I suppose that is the impression we're expected to go away with," Edith said. "But I don't see how we could have any other. The cameras don't lie. If that's freedom, they've changed the definition and they can have it."

Oren recalled Mark Olafson's words. No, he and Edith wouldn't like it out there.

The symphony went slowly for a time. But its progress was steady. Edith knew what she wanted to say through the music and she said it forcefully. Sometimes the statement came originally at her piano as she sat and coaxed the black and white keys to express a phrase that was throbbing through her body.

At other times whole passages suggested themselves to Edith with such clarity that the piano was superfluous.

The third movement was a revelation. The entire theme of it suggested itself to her in one brilliant mass as she was coming home from a department store sale. She was riding the moving pavement, clutching a few parcels she hadn't wanted to entrust to the delivery tubes and hemmed in by a crowd of other women shoppers. There, one flight underground, moving north at the speed of fifteen miles an hour and trying to ignore the advertising placards set into the tunnel ceiling at an angle just overhead, she felt the music hit her.

It came not as a phrase or snatch—not as a tender seedling thrusting hopefully through a crack it had made in the soil—but full-blown, like the bouquet of flowers a magician would produce from an empty fist.

The movement exploded in her mind, in a fraction of

a second, fully-developed. It was a natural outgrowth of the first and second movements, over which she had worked so hard, and, although it was similar to them thematically, it was a totally original concept of their potentials. It was as if the first two had mated and produced the third, spontaneously and perfectly.

Edith was transfixed as the music throbbed through her. She was carried two exits beyond her own before she realized it and then in her excitement elbowed her way to the slow lane and off, where she took the escalator to the street.

She walked home from there, quickly. She was running when the front door cushioned closed behind her. She threw the parcels to a couch, dropped her coat to the floor, sailed her hat across the room and was at the piano.

She was still at the piano, the floor around her littered with paper and pencil stubs and the ashtrays piled with cigaret butts, when her husband came home.

"Hi, Edie," he said. "How's the baby?"

She was irritated that his first thought should be of the child. But then she said:

"Oh my God! The baby!"

"What's the matter?" Oren asked. Alarmed, he headed for the nursery.

She followed him. "I plugged his sleeper into the sitter connection when I went shopping and when I came home—frankly I forgot all about him."

Martin was asleep, peacefully. If he was damp he didn't show it or object.

"What a terrible mother I am," Edith said. Anxiously she pressed a button and a voice said, almost instantly:

"Nursaway, Incorporated. Everything was just fine while you were gone. One moment, please."

That was just Tape A, but it did mean there had been no trouble; no need to send a nurse in person from the central sitter office.

"Electronic nursemaids," Oren snorted. He was about to elaborate when a viewscreen which could be seen from the baby's Sleeprplay went alight. The image of a young woman in a crisp white uniform appeared. She said:

"Martin was wonderful while you were gone. He slept most of the time. Once he got a bit cranky, but we ran off a puppet film on the screen, which amused him, and then played a Soothe-tune. He went back to sleep. You have a very fine baby, Mrs. Donn."

"Yes, I know," Edith said. "Thank you."

"Will there be anything else?"

"No. Thank you very much, Nurse."

"Thank you."

The screen darkened and Edith plugged out the connection.

"So everything's under control," Oren said. "I'll change him and feed him later, if you like." They went back to the studio. "You seem to be busy." He looked around at the mess.

She laughed and curled up on the couch, moving the parcels to the floor.

"You have no idea," she said. "I've been going like a mad one all afternoon. And the reason why? This will kill you." She spoke self-consciously. "Your strictly no-talent wife thinks she has something good. She thinks she has it and she may not lose it, if only she keeps working at it like fury so as to keep it from getting away."

"Of course you've got something," he said. "We both know that."

"But this is different. It's the third movement. It's all there. Part of it's down on paper—there," she pointed her chin at a mass of papers on the piano top, "and part of it's up here." She rapped her skull with her knuckles. "Or down here," she added. "I seem to feel it in my stomach, too. Is that the way great music is written—with the stomach?"

"I don't know," Oren said. "But if that's the way you write, that's the way you write."

"Well, this is ulcer music. Maybe I'll give it a name. Symphony Number 1 by Edith Donn, subtitled 'The Brain and the Ulcer.'"

"Good," he said. "Now you're relaxing. I'll get us a

drink and you knock off for the day so you can go at it fresh in the morning."

"Thanks," she said. "I'll take the drink, but I've got to get back to this. I can't risk losing it. If you don't mind getting your own supper, that is? I don't think I want anything."

He came back from the portable bar and handed her a drink.

"In the old days I'd have blown my stack," he said, grinning. "Work hard all day and then have to stand over a hot stove while my wife makes merry in the music room. But even though I'm Apologist Number One for the old-fashioned way, I must admit this modern cooking has grandma's methods beat all to hell."

"You know how to do it, don't you?" his wife asked. "The freezer's full of all kinds of meals. All you have to do . . ."

"I know," he said. "From the freezer into the Electronicook and onto the table in ten seconds flat. Then into me, and what's left into the Disposo. But just to be perverse, I think I'll have a couple of medieval sandwiches. If I fix you some and tiptoe in quietly with them, you'll eat them, won't you?"

"You're a darling," Edith said. She gave him a quick kiss and went to the piano. "Yes, I will."

At twenty-three thirty Oren Donn came out of the shower and peeked into the studio. Edith was still hard at work.

He wrote a note, tiptoed in and put it on the piano top:

"Baby's all tucked away. Now I'm tucking myself away. Please come to bed soon."

She read the note at a quick glance, smiled, blew him a kiss and nodded vaguely.

When he awoke the next morning the first thing he was conscious of was the muted sounds of the piano.

He went in to her.

"Honey, for God's sake!"

Her face was pale and drawn but her eyes were bright. She would play a few bars, then write a line of notes in quick, expert strokes. There was a little box of Tabodex on the piano top next to a glass.

"I'm fine," Edith said. "Don't worry about me. It's a bit tricky in spots, but it's really coming along."

"You've got to slow down—have some rest," he protested. "I won't let you do this to yourself."

"No," she said. "The music is more important. You run along. With luck, I'll be through with this movement by the time you're home."

He conceded defeat, respecting her judgment and sense of values as she had always respected his.

"All right, but don't overdo it. I'll make you some scrambled eggs and coffee. And I'm going to call Nursaway and get a sitter for Martin so you won't be disturbed. Except that she'll be instructed to feed you lunch—forcibly if necessary."

Edith put down her pencil, got to her feet, put her arms around him and rested her head on his chest.

"I just want to tell you," she said softly, "that you're the most wonderful, perfect, sensational, terrifically colossal person in the whole world and I love you love you love you love you." Her tears wet the skin of his chest in the V of his bathrobe. "Thank you for you," she whispered.

He kissed her on the top of her head and then on each wet cheek and gently on the mouth.

"Okay," he said, considerably affected. "Okay, fine. I'll go fix the eggs. And you write this thing good, Edie. Give it hell, Sweetheart. Give it hell."

Oren pushed open the door of the apartment that night and called:

"Edith. Edie!"

He went into the studio, but it was empty—and clean. The piano lid was down. The ashtrays were empty and sparkling. The papers were gone from the floor.

"Edie!" he cried.

A nurse in starched white came from the bedroom. She had her finger to her lips.

"What is it? What's the matter?"

"It's all right. Strain and fatigue is about all. I've given her a sedative and she's sleeping now. Dr. Harrons is on his way, but just as a precaution."

He pushed past the nurse and into the bedroom. Edith lay quietly in the center of the double bed, breathing just a bit heavily. He stood at the edge of the bed, looking at her.

The nurse followed him. She put her hand on Edith's forehead, in a gesture which she combined with the smoothing of the sleeping woman's hair, adjusted the covers and turned to smile at Oren.

"I'm sure there's nothing to worry about," she said.

"Poor kid," Oren said.

"I put her to bed," the nurse said. "And called you and the doctor. But as I said, it's just strain, I'm sure."

"Thank you, Miss Loring. I guess you didn't bargain for all this when you came to baby-sit."

"I'm glad I could help," she said. "Would you like me to fix you some coffee or anything while we wait for the doctor?"

"No, thanks. I'll go visit with Martin, I think, till he gets here. Has the baby been good?"

"Perfect," she said. "A real doll."

His son was asleep. Oren sat and looked at him and worried about Edith.

Doctor Harrons was packing his things away in his bag. He refused a drink but accepted one of Oren's cigarets and sat down in a straight-backed chair. Oren stood and fidgeted in front of him.

"It's as Miss Loring said." The doctor took out a prescription kit. "Fatigue, mostly. Your wife was driving herself on borrowed energy—she'd taken a few of those Tabodex things, you know. Perfectly all right, of course, occasionally, but you do have to let yourself catch up afterwards. Mrs. Donn just went a bit too far before allowing herself to catch up. A good night's rest and a minimum of activity tomorrow and she'll be as good as new. Who is your regular doctor?"

"We don't have one. We had Dr. Morales, but he was

just the obby—the obstetrician for the baby. A laboratory baby, of course."

"Good man, Morales, in his field. But I would suggest another in this case. I mean no criticism of Morales whatsoever, but he is a specialist. He'd be the first to tell you so himself. No, if I may make a recommendation, I'd say Dr. Leif."

"If you say so," Oren said. "I suppose you're too busy to take on another patient yourself?"

The doctor carefully ground out his cigaret in an ashtray. He looked at Oren, began a smile, then stopped it in the middle.

"Mr. Donn," he said, "apparently I have news for you. Have a drink yourself, Mr. Donn. Your wife is pregnant."

Oren stiffened. His face went through a series of contortions as it adjusted itself to the emotions chasing around behind it. He ended his confusion by breaking out into a broad grin.

"Pregnant!" he cried. "You mean pregnant? You mean she's going to have a baby? The way people used to do? The old-fashioned way? Naturally?"

"Naturally," said Dr. Harrons, grinning back.

"Oh, boy!" Oren exploded. "Oh, boy-oh-boy! That's wonderful!" He walked up and down the room in excitement. "Pregnant! Imagine that! The little devil! Doctor, I'm going to have a drink and you're going to have one with me."

"Well," the doctor said, "all right. Just a weak one."

Edith slept through the night.

Oren sent word to his office that he was taking the day off and he was anxiously hovering over his wife when she stirred into wakefulness.

"Hello, Maw," he said when her eyes opened.

"Hello, darling," she said. She stretched out a hand to him and he put it to his lips. It was warm and soft. "I feel so lazy and relaxed," she said.

"It's about time," he said. "And that's the way you're going to stay."

"Oh, but I can't. I have so much work to do. I've—" She frowned and looked around the sunlit room. "It's morning," she said. "I don't remember going to bed. What happened?"

"It's all right. Just relax."

"But it's not all right. I have work to do. I have to finish the symphony. I have a lot of work to do."

"You finished it," he said. "You finished it last night. Before I came home."

She frowned down at the covers. "I remember now. Yes, I did finish. But that was only the third movement. It was good. It came out all right, Oren. I remember. But I don't remember after that. Did I fall asleep in the studio?"

"Yes," he said. "And the babysitter put you to bed. You were knocked out."

"Well, I'm not knocked out any more. I've got to get right up and start the last movement. That's going to be a humdinger to tackle. I've got no ideas whatsoever. The third took everything out of me."

"So I hear," he said. "Now you listen to me. You're going to stay in bed all day. That's an order. Doctor's order. Maybe tonight, if you're very good, you can get up for a little while. But not before. You've got to take care of yourself. You owe it to the baby."

"Poor Marty. I've certainly been neglecting him. All right, I'll be good. I'll stay in bed and behave. And maybe you'll bring him in and he can stay with me, the way he's never had a chance to, in that damned old scientific box of his all the time.

"Edith Riordan Donn," he said to her, grinning. "Mrs. Oren Donn, I want you to stop talking like an idiot. The doctor has been here, and he's told me everything, and there's no point in your trying to hide it any longer because I know. I, your husband Mr. Donn. I know."

"Know what, silly? What doctor? What are you talking about?"

"You know perfectly well what I'm— Don't you? You mean you don't know? Don't you really?"

She laughed. "No, I don't. And if you keep mumbling

to yourself like a fool I never will. What are you talking about?"

He took both her hands in his and said:

"Edie, darling. The doctor was here. He examined you after you passed out. He said you'd been overworking yourself. He said you need a rest. But he also said— He said, and I think it's wonderful—he said we're going to have a baby."

She looked at him, her eyes wide.

"Oh, no!" she said.

She withdrew one of her hands and pulled it down the side of her face.

"Not no, yes. We're going to be real live parents. No bowl of mush stuff, with all due respect to Martin, but an honest-to-God old-fashioned baby."

Her staring eyes were focused on nothing. When she spoke again her voice was barely audible.

"Now, I'll never finish the symphony," she said. "It's no good any more. I can't do it now."

"Silly girl," he said. "You sound like Dr. Stern. Surely you can't agree with him now. You can have your baby and your symphony both. You can have a dozen babies and write a dozen symphonies, if you want to."

"No," she said dully. "Not now. I was talking a lot of bravado then. Now I'm just an ordinary woman, like all the rest. We can't do two things at once. We're strictly one-track people. It's our fate."

"Fate hell!" Oren exploded. "What a lot of nonsense you're talking. You did three movements, didn't you? You can do anything you want to do, if you'll only get out of this defeatist frame of mind."

"You're shouting at me." She looked at him, her eyes grown cold. "You did this thing to me and now you're shouting at me." Her voice rose and she had a wild look. "You're jealous of my work. I was doing something creative and you weren't and now you're jealous of my work and you're trying to destroy it. That's why I'm pregnant. You did it on purpose. You did it maliciously. Well, I won't let you destroy my music. I'll destroy your child first!"

She thrust the bedclothes aside and got unsteadily to her feet. He sprang up to help her. She shoved him aside, with more strength than he thought she possessed.

"Honey," he said.

"Hypocrite!" she yelled. She clawed a dress from a hanger in the closet, gathered together other clothing and ran to the bathroom, where she locked the door against him. He pounded on it.

"Edie," he said. "You're sick. Open the door. Come back to bed. I'll call the doctor."

"You needn't bother," she said. "I'm going to the doctor. I'm going to have an abortion."

Oren, pale and shaking, went to the communicator. He set it for private and whispered:

"Medical emergency."

A minute later the bathroom door opened and Edith came out, dressed for the street. Her face was ashen under its makeup. She carried her purse in her left hand and behind it she was shielding something she held in her right hand.

Oren stood at the front door, barring her way.

"You're not going out," he said softly. "Please, darling, be reasonable."

She walked toward him. She lifted the purse so he could see the large pair of scissors in her other hand, the point of one blade just touching her body.

"Open the door, my dear husband," she said. "Let me go out."

He hesitated only a moment, watching her mad eyes, then opened the door for her.

They brought her back on a stretcher ten minutes late. She was unconscious. At Oren's gesture the two men carrying the stretcher took it into the bedroom and the young medical officer with the gold badge on his white tunic helped them transfer her to the bed.

"Preventive paralysis," the officer said to Oren. "She's all right. We tracked her from the street door as soon as we got your call and made contact in person a minute or two later."

"But you had to use the para ray?" Oren asked.

"She was carrying those shears and we couldn't take a chance. She seemed to be wandering aimlessly until she began to run and we pre-parred her. No one saw and Dr. Soames caught her as she fell. There'll be no publicity, I think I can assure you."

"Thank God for that." Oren knelt by the bed and pushed a lock of hair away from his wife's face. She was breathing peacefully and the mad look had gone.

"There will be a few questions, though, if we can go into the next room. Dr. Soames will see that Mrs. Donn is made comfortable."

"Questions?"

"Just routine," the medical officer said. "For the department records. Confidential, of course." He took Oren's elbow and guided him out of the bedroom.

The questions, if routine, were extensive. At one point Oren angrily crushed out a cigaret and said:

"What is this, anyway? You make it sound like a police matter. If we're charged with anything let me know and I'll get a lawyer. I don't like this inquisition."

"Well, now," soothed the medical officer, "you know that there's often a very fine line of demarcation between a medical case and a police matter. Our department must have the facts if the case is to be closed."

"Don't call it a 'case.' You make me sorry I ever called you."

"You might have been sorrier if you hadn't," the officer said coldly, his affability slipping for a moment. "Our job is to safeguard all the citizenry and it's people like you who make things difficult."

Oren jumped to his feet.

"Listen, you young squirt," he began. But Soames came from the bedroom then and after a grave look at Oren whispered into the officer's ear.

The medical officer frowned.

"What is it?" asked Oren. "What's wrong?"

"Mr. Donn," the officer said reproachfully, "you didn't tell us your wife was pregnant."

"You didn't give me a chance to, with your stupid questions. Well, what of it?"

"We should have had that fact in our possession at the time we answered your emergency call," the officer said sententiously. "Then we would have proceeded differently. As it is, you must take responsibility."

"Responsibility for what? What do you mean?"

"I mean this. Preventive paralysis is harmless, generally speaking, but its effect on a foetus or embryo is not completely known and may even be harmful. Therefore we disclaim responsibility for any injury or mutation which may occur in the course of this natural birth. I have a form here which I must ask you to sign, to absolve the departm—"

That was when Oren socked him in the jaw.

It was thirty-six hours before the Donn household was back nearly to normal.

Oren had been under house arrest for twenty-four of those hours. During that time the house had been aswarm with Council Guards, medics and medical officers, a lawyer, nurses, a baby-sitter and reporters from half a dozen news media. One reporter carrying a creepy-peepy sent the scene out for triveo.

Finally all of them had gone except Oren's lawyer, in whose custody he was paroled.

"Not only don't they have a case, Oren," the lawyer said, "but you might have a strong action against the Council. I say this in the strictly legal sense, of course, without consideration of such extra-legal little gimmicks such as Suggestions and Resolutions they could whip out at the spur of a moment, and assuming that they'd allow a suit. I imagine, though, that all you want is peace and privacy again."

"Exactly, Burt," Oren said. He kicked at a fax tabloid whose headline screamed:

"MUSIC HER BABY"—SCISSOR PSYCHO

"You could sue that sheet, at least," Burt said.

"Forget it."

The bedroom door opened. Oren pushed the tabloid under the couch with his toe as he got to his feet.

Edith came in, wearing a hostess gown and smiling uncertainly.

"Hello, darling," she said. "Hello, Burt. I've been a bad girl, haven't I?"

Oren went to her and led her to the couch. She was a bit unsteady on her feet. She relaxed gratefully.

"We're not going to talk about anything unpleasant tonight," her husband said. "We'll pretend that Burt is here on one of his rare social evenings."

They pretended as best they could but it was not a success. Oren was worried about his wife's condition and was not talkative. Edith, who had not been told there was anything to worry about, was pale under her makeup and wore a fixed half-smile which soon choked off Burt's attempts at conversation.

So in desperation they switched on the triveo.

It was Jerry Hilarious night and the scarlet-haired comedian was in rare form.

His material usually was topical, and tonight it was right up to the minute. They had turned him on in the middle of a routine which obviously was a parody of the Donn case. Since they had missed the beginning, it wasn't too clear what was going on, but in the act with Jerry Hilarious were a couple wearing heavy glasses—which he had made symbolic of the intellectuals the City-State so despised. Moreover, the girl was wearing as a costume a print dress polka-dotted with music notes and a hat that was a grand piano, while the man, obviously a snob, carried a heavy old-fashioned book under his arm.

"Oh, he's subtle," said Burt. "Subtle as a kick in the teeth. Shall I turn him off?"

"No," said Oren. "We might as well see ourselves as The Common Man sees us—unless it upsets you, Edie?"

"It's all right," she said. "It has a certain fascination."

The triveo couple, with Jerry Hilarious laughing it up in the foreground, were singing:

"We don't like the City-State
   But we think *we* are just first rate."

The couple, with their faces fixed in expressions of the utmost gravity, were going through a series of insane antics as they sang the verses, and the studio audience was roaring with laughter as Jerry Hilarious mugged, cross-eyed, and danced around the pair with his arms and legs flailing fantastically.

The production ended with a crash of music and a sudden silence in which Jerry Hilarious wound up and let fly his gesture of banishment.

"Aw, g'wan *outside!*" he cried.

A wind machine went into action and, as it howled, snowflakes pelted the ridiculous, bespectacled couple. They cringed away from the gesture and crept toward an icy gate.

Edith, with a switch next to the couch, cut off the triveo. Her expression was angry and her lips were pressed into a firm line.

"You know," she said, "I'd like to do just that."

The doctors—both the Health Department experts and the Donns' private physician—couldn't tell what the effect of the para ray would be on Edith's unborn child. It was alive, they agreed, but whether it would be normal after birth was something they could not yet say. They put her through a Diagnosticon, they thumped on her belly with fingers and X-steths, they examined smears and slides and dials and they said they'd be back to run some more tests when she was five months pregnant. It was thoroughly humiliating.

Oren was tried on the assault charge. The trial was held in chambers with the press barred. Nothing had appeared anywhere about the fact that Edith was pregnant when she was rayed down by preventive paralysis and the Council intended that nothing should.

The case was handled as one of simple assault and the judge sentenced Oren to a year in Correction, then suspended the sentence. He was free then, but from that time on the Donns were under surveillance.

They planned one Restday to go on a gyro trip with a picnic lunch. They hadn't ever made such a trip as a family unit, and little Marty seemed to sense their anticipation. His heels kicked against the lunch pack as they wheeled him the few blocks to the gyropark. But the plane wasn't there. A hostile attendant, speaking from the back of his booth as if fearing contamination, told them the Council Guards had confiscated it.

Marty sensed their mood of frustration and bitterness as they wheeled him back home and he began to cry. He was still crying when they reached the house and Oren on an angry impulse put the infant in the Sleeprplay and cut off his yowls by turning the soundproof switch. Then Oren went into the study and turned on the artificial rain; the streams of water slammed against the window. But suddenly the sound stopped. He looked up and saw a Council Guard looking at him from outside the panes. The booted, green-tunicked guard motioned to him to open the window.

He did, and asked belligerently, "Did you turn that off?"

"I did," the guard said. "As you must be aware, there's a Suggestion against artificial rain. In addition to being wasteful, it's naturalistic."

The guard took out a pocket Listener and aimed it at Oren.

"I didn't know about any such Suggestion," Oren said. He was leaning out the window and talking loudly to the guard standing in the garden below. "And if there is such a Suggestion, it's petty tyranny."

"Oren Donn, with two n's," the guard said into the Listener. "And 'tyranny.' That was the word you used, wasn't it, Mr. Donn?"

"Go to hell," exploded Oren. "And get the hell out of my garden. You have no right here at all."

"And use of profanity to a guard in the performance

of his duty," the guard said. "People under surveillance are subject to loss of certain rights. I'm sure that was explained to you at the time of your trial."

Oren bit the inside of his cheek then, and was silent. The guard looked up at Oren, smiled faintly and put the Listener back in his pocket.

"Nothing else to say, Mr. Donn? Too bad. I was enjoying your lecture, as I am sure the Council will when it is transcribed for them. Nice garden you have here. Very natural."

The guard turned and on his way to the gate at the back of the garden his heavy boots tramped through a border of moss roses.

Oren bit off a little piece of the inside of his cheek.

A man had been standing in the street beyond the garden, watching the scene, and he walked on leisurely as the guard left. The guard gave him a passing glance and disappeared around a corner. Oren recognized the man. Mark Olafson, the man from Outside. Oren was about to speak when Mark shook his head almost imperceptibly. Then he, too, disappeared from view.

At his office the next day Oren spent the entire morning failing to get anything accomplished. Half a dozen times he began to tackle the correspondence that had accumulated over the weekend and half a dozen times he yanked the page out of the voicewriter. He was still in his mood when the reception screen showed that he had a visitor. It was Mark Olafson, but the name he gave now was Ross Buckley and his appearance was that of a successful businessman.

Oren looked his surprise.

"Well," he said. "Made a go of it, have you?"

"You might say so," Mark replied. "In a manner of speaking."

"I saw you go by our place yesterday, but I had no idea you'd had such a complete change of fortune. Why didn't you come in? Or is that a stupid question? I'm not much of a conspirator."

"You're not a conspirator at all, I'm afraid," Mark

said. He lifted a flap in Oren's desk and pressed the button that wiped the conversation tape. "You'll pardon me. No, Donnie, you're just a victim of an evil, stupid goverment. I saw that little drama in the garden yesterday, and I know more about you and Edith than you might suppose—never mind how. I've been busy since you and I last talked. In several ways. And I know that things have changed with you."

"They have, Mar—Buckley. They certainly have."

"Good lad. Thanks for the 'Buckley.' We'll make a conspirator of you yet."

"They're driving me into it," Oren said. "Or out of the City-State, at any rate. Edith is already half-way thinking about that Jerry Hilarious thing as being a good idea—that 'g'wan outside' business. I guess you've been here long enough now to know about Jerry Hilarious."

"Yes," said Mark. "I've become very well acclimated. You know, Donnie, once I told you I didn't think you'd like it out there. Now I'm not so sure. It hasn't changed any Outside, except insofar as it's always changing—for the better, we think—but . . ."

"I know," Oren said. "I've changed. I'm waking up."

Mark Olafson looked at the other man intently. "I shouldn't do this," he said. "It's not my primary job, directly. But if you like, I'll help you go."

"Oh?" Oren chewed his lip for a while. "I'd like to think about it, and talk to Edith. Could we make a living? We're not farmers or laborers, you know. And—could we take it?"

"Yes, to both. I suppose you've been saturated with the propaganda films about Outside. I'll not tell you they're fakes, because they're not exactly. They're factual as far as they go. But they only go as far with their cameras and spies as we let them go."

"Oh?" Oren said again. "You mean there's more than—"

"Lots more. I think I can safely say—to you—that you'd be pleasantly surprised. Some of our people are farmers, of course, and some work in factories. But we have a thing called a Constitution, pretty much the same as the one a bunch of the boys hammered out back in the seventeen hundreds. It says things, for instance, about freedom of the press, and that means books, and books means somebody has to publish them."

"Books?" said Oren.

"Of course. Your business. Ours don't talk, yet. You still have to turn the pages and know how to read. But it's something you could do if you didn't mind going into the print shop once in a while and getting your hands inky."

"Printer's ink," said Oren. "How I used to love that smell! But how about Edith's music?"

"We're not barbarians, except maybe when the City-State turns its cameras on us. We have music, too."

"Well." Oren's eyes had a far-off look in them.

"Well?" Mark echoed the word, smiling.

"I don't know what to say. I'm tempted, very much, to pack right up and move out there, but I don't know. This is my country, even if it's wrong in a lot of ways, and maybe I should stay and try to help make it right instead of deserting it."

"That's a noble thought. I don't mean that flippantly," Mark added quickly. "I respect you for it. But can the few people like you who are left still do anything—from Inside?"

"I don't know," Oren said. "I'll have to think about it."

"I'll be around," Mark said. "Now that I'm respectable, or almost, I'll be keeping in touch with you."

"Good. What are you doing here—as Ross Buckley, I mean?"

"Officially—at least as far as the City-State is concerned—I'm in the talking book business. Just like you. That's why it'll be easy for me to see you often, after I've really got started. Unofficially—you might say I'm in the business of counter-propaganda, or recruiting."

Oren realized that he'd be no use in the office the rest of the day, either, and decided to go home and talk to Edith.

"You'd better let me go ahead, by about five minutes," Mark said. "I don't think we should be seen together in public until things have firmed up just a bit more."

Oren never saw him again. When he reached the street he found a crowd of people watching the departure of a Council Guard van. He asked the doorman what had happened.

"They got an Outsider. He puts up a struggle but they beats him over the head and takes him off."

With his stomach squeezed tight Oren asked, "Where did he come from?"

"Somewheres in the building. Just by luck the same elevator jockey brings him down as takes him up and remembers the floor he comes from. The guards are up there now. They got the whole thirty-sixth floor sealed off and every last soul up there is getting their heads grilled off."

Mark Olafson must have walked three flights before and after his visit. Oren's office was on the thirty-ninth floor.

Mark's arrest brought new tension into the Donn home. Oren knew Mark would never mention his name but he was frightened by the efficiency of the Council Guard in tracking down the Outsider despite his elaborate precautions. Apparently no one but the mechanical reception screen had seen Mark visit his office and fortunately it was not one that kept a permanent record. But presumably they knew where Mark Olafson lived and the clothes Oren had brought for him might be traced, if Mark had kept them.

Although Oren tried to keep his new worry from Edith, she finally forced it from him. But with it went the picture of Outside as Mark had described it for him and that, at least, was a consolation. The couple talked more and more seriously about making the break with their once-comfortable life and fleeing to the wilderness that now seemed more a promise of paradise. But where once they could have made the emigration with no difficulty other than the scorn of their friends and the sneers of a government which would have confiscated their funds as it stamped their visas, they now were trapped in a land they had come to loathe. As a man under surveillance, Oren had only limited freedom. They'd already taken his gyro and he was sure that if he strayed far from the route between his home and office he'd soon be tapped on the shoulder by a Council Guard.

In this atmosphere Edith's music stagnated. It was an academic question now whether the fact that she was naturally pregnant meant that she could not write a great symphony. She knew she could not write a bar now if she was a sixteenth generation obby baby whose female ancestors for three hundred years had been born in bowls of laboratory mush.

Then, in the fifth month of her pregnancy, the Health Department specialists came back for the reexamination. All the exhaustive tests again were made but still there was none among them who could say with any certainty if Edith's child would be normal after birth. Preventive paralysis was a tricky thing. That was about all they could state positively, and there had been only a few cases of an expectant mother having been pre-parred.

The specialists went into a conference and emerged with a Recommendation which they sent to the City-State Council. The Council deliberated and issued a Suggestion to Mr. and Mrs. Oren Donn.

A Suggestion to a person under surveillance had the power of a Resolution and, of course, a Resolution was an Edict, backed by whatever force was needed to carry it out.

The Suggestion was that the mother should enter a Health Department hospital at the beginning of her ninth month and be subject to exhaustive tests under rigidly-controlled conditions. Then, if it was indicated that the birth would be normal—if something so old-fashioned as a natural birth could be considered "normal" —a film record would be made of the birth and of the infant's progress.

It would of course be necessary to have a complete record until such time as the child was found to be either normal or abnormal and therefore it was suggested that the child would become a ward of the City-State while doubt remained. The mother would be free to return home after the birth.

That was when Oren and Edith decided they'd had it. They read the copy of the Suggestion which had been brought to them for their signatures. They signed it, received the thanks of the medical officer for their intelligent cooperation, and then made their plans.

There was to be, on the Restday after next, the annual Rededication Jubilee in State Square, a vast public amphitheater. It was the one day in the year when the Members of the Council made a public appearance and of course everyone went to pay his respects and add to the din of applause and cheers when the Members made their brief speeches. It was also the day awards were made in the form of medals and scrolls to citizens who had done most for the City-State during the preceding year. Mostly the recipients were officials of the government, but they never were the Council Members themselves, who year after year modestly refused their nomination by the awards committee.

This alone should have been enough to guarantee attendance, but there was always entertainment besides. The greatest names in the movies and triveo appeared, each with a special new act never before seen anywhere. The star of stars this year was to be Jerry Hilarious, that sensational new triveo comic.

There was no triveo of the Jubilee, however. It was thoroughly understood that it would be unpatriotic not to be one of the crowd personally taking part in the Oath of Rededication that climaxed the occasion. Therefore there would be no one at home to see a triveo cast of it. Films were made, though, for showing at a later date to those who had to work on the holiday and those in institutions.

Jubilee Day dawned hot and sunny. Oren and Ethel knew that their best chance would come when the ceremonies ended and the mobs of people swarmed in all directions for home. They and little Marty in his baby buggy would be part of that anonymous crowd and they would let that part of it which swarmed west take them with it—toward the setting sun, and Outside. Just exactly how they would escape notice when they reached the outskirts of the City-State, or how they would cross the boundary, they did not know. But if there was a way they would find it.

It was a long day. They'd taken nothing with them except some changes of clothing for the baby, and only as much money as they would normally be expected to carry with them, and Edith's music—the manuscript of the first three movements of her symphony. But though they were traveling light they had the weight of fear with them until they had worked themselves well into the center of the crowd in the great square. They found seats.

Under the broiling sun—the heat only slightly mitigated by the frigeration towers—the program began. The vast audience was restless despite the brevity of the official speeches but when each ended the applause was deafening. Oren and Edith applauded, too, looking cautiously around to see if any guards were watching. None was in sight anywhere near them.

Jerry Hilarious romped onto the stage and was welcomed with a roar of laughter. At first the Donns forced themselves to laugh at his antics, not to seem out of place, and as they watched they realized that the short, wiry redhead was genuinely an artist and not just a buffoon.

He was giving a masterful performance and through his special material could be seen the man, warm-hearted, inventive, instantly responsive to the mood of the crowd. Oren and Edith relaxed and felt their tension ease off. They gained strength through the respite for the journey ahead. Only when Jerry Hilarious wound himself up and threw his familiar catch line at the crowd did Edith fail to laugh.

"Aw," boomed the words, "g'wan *outside!*"

"Amen," said Edith under her breath.

Finally, after repeated encores, Jerry Hilarious left the stage. Act after act followed and at last, in late afternoon, the program ended with the solemn Oath of Rededication. The Donns mouthed the promissory, meaningless words, stood up from the folding chairs for the recessional music and then joined a throng that was heading west.

The crush was so great that Oren took Marty up and carried him while Edith collapsed the baby buggy to briefcase size and carried it. They found a kiosk and, surrounded by humanity, made their way down to the westbound moving pavement. Clinging together so as not to lose each other, they were propelled along at a steady fifteen miles an hour.

The pavement and the throng took them under the Hudson River and into what had once been New Jersey but which now was just another part of Greater New York. The crowd had begun to thin as the pavement branched north and south but there were still many thousands of people heading west. Marty was asleep with his head on his father's shoulder and Oren's arms were beginning to ache. Edith had a pain in the back of the neck, as if someone were staring at her there and any moment would tap her on the shoulder and say "Go back."

Miles later the moving pavement ended, at the top of a rise. Nearby was a loading platform for buses. Neither of them knew where they were or in which direction to go next.

A dilapidated old gasoline bus that still carried the lettering *Pennsylvania Greyhound* was marked *Borderville* and they boarded that one.

They were exhausted when the bus reached its terminal. It had been crowded when it started off. The Donns had found seats but many others stood. At the

end of the line, however, less than two dozen persons
still were ~~cleared~~

Wearily the Donns got up. When they left the bus
it drove off. Their fellow riders melted away into the
dusk and the Donns walked at random down a street
of ancient houses and old-fashioned stores with full
plate-glass windows. They tried to look as if they had
a destination.

Several blocks later they saw a sign in red neon tubing,
which once had spelled HOTEL. They would have
to go in. They could do nothing more tonight.

In the dimly lit lobby, an old man sat in a heavy armchair behind the counter, dozing. There was no one
else.

Oren cleared his throat and the man opened his
eyes.

"Hi, there," he said. "Customers, eh? Always get a
customer or two on Jubilee Day. How was the show?"

"Great," said Oren without enthusiasm. "Could we
have a double room, please, with an extra cot for the
baby? I don't suppose you have a crib."

"Sure do," the old man said. "We ain't so antiquated
as you think, though we are a mite far off from the
center of things. Like a room with a bath, or would
down the hall do you? Five credits cheaper for down the
hall."

"With bath, please," Oren smiled. He couldn't remember that he'd ever had to make the choice before.

"Right you are, sir. Sir," he repeated. "Sometimes forget to say that." He cackled. "You from Outside? Or
maybe goin' there? I know you ain't from around here."

Edith looked at Oren with weary, frightened eyes and
Marty whimpered sleepily as Oren shifted him to the
other shoulder.

The old man cackled again. "That's all right," he said.
"You don't have to say nothin'. Lots of Outsiders sneak
across on Jubilee Day. And vicey versa. Nobody pays
much mind. I certainly ain't goin' to make a fuss about
it. All I care about's you pay me twenty credits in advance, seein' as you got no luggage."

Oren fished out his wallet and handed it to Edith, who counted out twenty credits to the old man, who put them in his pocket and took a key out of a cubbyhole.

"Second floor," he said. "Elevator got cranky couple years ago and it ain't worked since. Hope you don't mind the stairs."

The stairs creaked loudly as they climbed them. Their room was just off the stair well and there was a film of dust on the battered chest of drawers. When Edith took the spread off the big double bed, though, she found fresh linen underneath. Oren put the baby down with a grunt of relief.

"I'll bring the crib up in a little while," the old man said. "Anything else you'd like?" He was dubious when Oren asked about the possibility of having a meal sent up to the room but finally agreed to see what he could do. Maybe the place down the street, if they weren't too busy. He went out.

The food came sooner than they had dared hope. It was hot and good although they had to eat off a rickety card table the old man brought up with the crib.

They ate the meal, fed the baby and put him to bed and then, while Edith ran herself a hot bath, Oren went down to the lobby to buy cigarets.

The stairs creaked under his feet but the sound was drowned out by a crash as the street door was thrown open and a crowd of people entered in a babble of loud talk. There were about a dozen of them. Two of them were women and all of them seemed to be drunk. All were well dressed.

Oren froze on the landing, half in the shadow. He dared not go back up for fear of attracting attention to himself, so he stood and watched.

One man, apparently the leader of the noisy group, went to the counter and pounded on it.

"Innkeeper!" he commanded. He took off his hat and sailed it neatly onto the branch of a coat-tree across the room. The gesture revealed a flaming shock of red hair. There was no doubt of his identity.

Jerry Hilarious.

Oren drew himself farther back into the corner of the landing.

The old man came around a corner of the lobby.

"There you are," said Jerry Hilarious. "Throw open the bar for these good people, Innkeeper. They're beginning to run down."

"Ain't got no bar, strictly speakin'," the old man said.

"I have hung up my hat and I intend to stay," the red-haired man said. "You have tables in the lobby. These will do. Put liquor on them. Or would you rather"—he wound up and let fly his gesture of banishment at the old man—"g'wan *outside!*"

One of the other men in the group slapped a third on the back and howled:

"That Jerry Hilarious—he kills me!"

The old man spat calmly into a flaked enamel cuspidor. "Don't kill me," he said. "If you got money I guess I can rustle up some bar whisky from someplace. We get all kinds here. You come from the Jubilee, I take it?"

A florid-faced man in a checkered tunic pushed importantly forward and slapped some credits on the counter. "Take it!" he cried, laughing drunkenly. "We brought the Jubilee with us—hah, Jerry?"

"I have brought this roistering company," Jerry Hilarious said, "to see the outside of the Outside. But if you don't hurry they'll start to unroister, which is a disheartening sight. So hasten with the liquor, Innkeeper."

The comedian ended his little speech with a crazy dance that evoked more laughter. The old man brought bottles and glasses from under the counter and set them out on the tables. One of the women hiccupped in a moment of silence and leaned against her escort for support.

"Music!" cried Jerry Hilarious. "Turn on the triveo!"

"Trivia!" shouted the man in the checkered tunic. "Turn on the trivia!"

"Sir," said Jerry Hilarious, pirouetting and jabbing a

finger into one of the checks, "you slander my profession. G'wan outside!"

"G'wan outside! G'wan outside!" the others echoed, laughing, and the company was roistering again.

"Ain't got no triveo," the old man said without apology. "Got an old video, though." He switched it on.

"I don't think this is a very good party," said the woman who had hiccuped. "I'm depressed."

"Can't expect all the conveniences, dear, when you get so far from civilization," her escort said. "Can you, Jerry?"

"Extemporaneous reply," Jerry Hilarious said. He sang:

> You'd feel worse in a hearse—
> You'd be drab on a slab.
> That is the curse
> Of being inside the Outside.

He went into one of his fantastic dances as music blasted out of the video.

Oren took advantage of the diversion to slip back upstairs and into their room.

Edith came out of the bathroom with a towel wrapped around her.

"What's all that noise, Oren?" she asked. "It worried me."

"It's Jerry Hilarious, of all people. He's got a crowd with him on the tail end of some private Jubilee."

"Jerry Hilarious!" she said. "Did they see you?"

"I don't think so."

"Why did they come all the way out here?" she asked.

"Educational tour, apparently. Slumming to see how it is in borderland so they can congratulate themselves on living where they do. We can't leave. About all we can do is try to get some sleep and see what happens in the morning. I don't think they'll make a night of it. A couple of them are pretty bored already."

But an hour later, as they were dozing off, they heard the stairs creak.

It wasn't the tired tread of the old man. Someone was taking the steps two at a time. They listened in alarm to the footsteps, then in dread as they stopped just outside their door. There was a knock, a brisk tattoo.

They dressed quickly. Oren opened the door.

Jerry Hilarious stood there.

Oren's heart sank. Edith came to his side.

"Oh," she said. She took Oren's hand.

"Hello," Jerry Hilarious said. He was smiling. "May I come in? I could only get away for a minute."

"So you found us," Oren said in despair. He opened the door wider, then closed it behind the comedian.

"And we were laughing at you—with you, really—just this afternoon," Edith said. "I know you have to work for them that way, but I didn't think you were their bloodhound, too."

"No, no," said Jerry Hilarious. "I've never hunted anything, except laughs. I'm sorry if I frightened you. I'm on your side, the way Mark Olafson was."

"You know Mark?" Oren asked.

"I knew him. He's dead. They beat him to death. They'd beat me to death, too, if they found out about me."

"Then you're an Outsider, too?" Oren asked. Relief swept through him.

Edith grasped the comedian's hand. "Mr. Hilarious," she said. "Oh, I could cry."

"Call me Jerry. That's my real name. The Hilarious is strictly for laughs."

"Poor Mark," Oren said. "It was my fault. They killed him because he tried to help us."

"No," said Jerry. "It had nothing to do with you. He told us about you, but they never knew of any connection, either way. Mark slipped up somewhere along the line, or they were too clever for him. It's a chance we all take.

"We volunteer to go in. To infiltrate the system and

1elp point up its evils and contradictions to intelligent
3eople—people like you."

"You had me fooled," Oren said. "But in the end it
was that crazy gag line of yours that we remembered
—and we went."

"You certainly did," Jerry said. "You went a lot
sooner than we expected you to and we had the devil's
own time finding you. I come here every Jubilee Day—
guiding a tour of drunks from Inside makes fine camou-
flage. It's a sort of wide-open town anyway and I can
report and get new instructions from Outside. The old
man told me you were here. He's one of us."

"I liked him, too," Oren said. "How many of you
are there, Inside?"

"Plenty of us. There have to be, because there are a
lot of you—people we need Outside."

"You *need* us?" Edith asked. "Honestly? We're not
just—refugees?"

"You're a *cause celebre*," Jerry said. "And in that
connection I think I can reassure you about your baby,
Mrs. Donn." Edith looked toward the crib where Marty
was sleeping. "The new one," Jerry said. "We've had
experience with the para-ray and your baby will be all
right."

"Thank God," said Edith.

"And of course we need you," Jerry went on. "We're
rebuilding from nothing. We've got willing hands and
stout hearts but we need a brain or two besides. And a
little music to lighten the burden, Mrs. Donn.

"We want to live in peace with the City-States, even
though we're the remnants of their defeated enemies.
But if we can't live side by side in dignity and if it
comes to a struggle, one day there'll be a lightning coup
from within and without simultaneously. As I said,
there are many of us, and some of us are pretty high up."

"Do you mean in the government itself?" Oren asked.

Jerry smiled. "I've talked too much already. And I
have to get back to the roisterers. Now go to sleep.
Talk to the old man in the morning, and he'll send you
to a man who'll show you the way."

As he left them, Jerry Hilarious said softly, smiling and without the gesture:

"G'wan outside!"

As they walked, the next morning, towards sanity and dignity, the sun came out. It was warm and friendly.

Edith felt a slight movement of life inside her.

Maybe she'd never write the fourth movement of her symphony now, but she didn't care. She was beginning to live it.